UNLEASHED
RETRIBUTION

SIGMUND BROUWER

ORCA BOOK PUBLISHERS

Copyright © 2015 Sigmund Brouwer

Library and Archives Canada Cataloguing in Publication

Brouwer, Sigmund, 1959–, author
Unleashed / Sigmund Brouwer.
(Retribution)

Issued in print and electronic formats.
ISBN 978-1-4598-0730-3 (pbk.).— ISBN 978-1-4598-0732-7 (pdf).—
ISBN 978-1-4598-0733-4 (epub)

I. Title. II. Series: Retribution (Victoria, B.C.)
PS8553.R68467U55 2015   jC813'.54   C2015-901716-5
C2015-901717-3

First published in the United States, 2015
Library of Congress Control Number: 2015935523

Summary: Jace has taken up boxing on the wrong side of the tracks as
he prepares to seek vengeance on his abusive father with two other
teen vigilantes in this fast-paced entry in the Retribution trilogy.

*Orca Book Publishers is dedicated to preserving the environment and has
printed this book on Forest Stewardship Council® certified paper.*

Orca Book Publishers gratefully acknowledges the support for its publishing
programs provided by the following agencies: the Government of Canada
through the Canada Book Fund and the Canada Council for the Arts,
and the Province of British Columbia through the BC Arts Council
and the Book Publishing Tax Credit.

Cover image by iStock.com
Author photo by Curtis Comeau

ORCA BOOK PUBLISHERS
www.orcabook.com

Printed and bound in Canada.

18 17 16 15 • 4 3 2 1

As always and forever,
for Savannah and Olivia.

ONE

THERE IS NO ONE AROUND TO HEAR YOU SCREAM.

The words came into focus as I woke up on a toilet. The last thing I remembered was drinking Gatorade. Then a fog that had turned into midnight black.

Someone had dragged my unconscious body from the back of the mildewy gym where I'd passed out to the bathroom of the locker room, where I found myself now.

I was bound with duct tape. I was still in my sweats, sitting on top of the toilet-seat lid. Those factors, at least, were a small mercy. One, being in sweats, and two, on the lid of the toilet seat as opposed to the seat itself. After not knowing how you got there and being unable to move, it would be even more awkward to look down and see your sweatpants bunched at your ankles.

The duct tape kept me from moving. I had no idea who had done this to me. The logical guess was the owner of a pair of white leather Converse basketball shoes on the floor on the other side of the cubicle door, toes facing me as if he were about to push open the door to use the toilet. I guessed it was a he only because the shoes looked like size twelve. Doubtful they would be a female's, unless she was clever enough to put on shoes that large to fool me. After I gave that some thought, it struck me that it could be possible, because another short-term difficulty I'd been facing had been caused by Jo and Raven, two girls my age who were genius, demented freaks. Maybe they'd had something to do with this.

The note was taped to the inside of the door at eye level. It was clearly meant for me to read when I awoke. Given that I was barely recovering from whatever had been slipped into the Gatorade, it was good that the computer-printed letters were in caps for visibility.

THERE IS NO ONE AROUND TO HEAR YOU SCREAM.

True. Terrifyingly true.

Before waking up on the toilet-seat lid, I'd been the last person in the gym, listening to the echoes of my knuckles slamming into a punching bag. Billy, who owned the place, trusted me enough to give me a set of keys to lock up and set the security. And it was trust. This gym meant the world to Billy, and it was a responsibility I took seriously. Billy might have been more relaxed if he knew that the place could burn down and my father would simply write a check to replace the entire building, and that the amount would be covered by the interest made in less than a month by my trust fund. But Billy didn't know that, and I wanted it to stay that way. To Billy, I was just another kid on the streets, clawing for a way out of Vancouver's inner city. To me, this was my escape, my outlet for the rage that I woke up with every morning.

ANSWER MY QUESTIONS, OR YOU WILL NEVER BOX AGAIN.

Obviously, then, I was here because the person who had done this expected that I would not want to answer the questions. Otherwise, why not just walk up to me and ask? The threat on the note also told me that the person on the other side of the cubicle door knew me well enough to know how much boxing meant to me.

AFTER A CURLING IRON HEATS UP, IT STAYS HOT FOR TWENTY MINUTES AND THEN AUTOMATICALLY SHUTS OFF. AFTER IT COOLS DOWN, IF IT IS STILL PLUGGED IN, IT BEGINS TO HEAT UP AGAIN. I WILL STAY HERE ALL NIGHT LISTENING TO YOU SCREAM IF YOU DON'T GIVE ME THE ANSWERS.

In my other world, I play chess. People think I'm smart. That's nothing that makes me proud. That's just a matter of hitting a genetic lottery jackpot, although most of the time it seems more like a curse than a blessing, just like the other world I was born into. I was more proud of what I'd done in my chosen world. How I'd endured countless hours toughening my hands against a punching bag. It didn't take a genius to understand the implications of the part of the note about the curling irons.

Each of my hands was taped to a curling iron. Once the curling irons were plugged in, the skin on the inside of my fingers and on my palms would melt with third-degree burns. The heat would go away when the curling irons shut off. Then I'd sit here in agony, smelling my burnt flesh, waiting for the curling irons to cool down and then automatically start up again.

CALL OUT WHEN YOU ARE READY, AND I WILL ASK THE FIRST QUESTION.

The fact that the notes were printed, not handwritten, showed that this had been planned. I assumed by the person in the white leather Converse shoes. There was a deep scratch in the leather, across the toe of the left shoe. A clue, right?

The person on the other side of the door knocked politely. I didn't respond. I had shifted focus to my hands and how tightly my fingers were wrapped around the curling irons. With my upper body, I leaned away from the wall to try to pull at the duct tape that was holding me to the pipes. That made just enough noise to tell the person who owned the basketball shoes that I was now awake.

A pad of yellow, lined paper made it over the door. There was a small hole at the top of the pad where a nail or drill had pierced it, and fishing line had been tied through the hole of the pad. The block printing on this one was handwritten.

I HEARD YOU MOVE SO I KNOW YOU ARE AWAKE. ARE YOU READY TO TALK?

I stayed silent.

The pad disappeared as the person on the other side tugged on the fishing line and pulled it up and over the door again.

This was so eerie. Except for the dripping of a leaky faucet, silence. Just me. Someone on the other side of the door. And then another new noise, which was the ripping off of the top sheet of paper from the pad, followed by the scratching of pencil on paper. The pad appeared again, sliding down the inside of the toilet door.

OKAY THEN. I'M GOING TO PLUG IN THE CURLING IRONS. TRUST-FUND MONEY WON'T PROTECT YOU HERE.

The pad disappeared.

I heard footsteps on the tiled floor. The extension cord at the end of the curling-iron cords wiggled slightly. I heard a clicking sound at the far wall, the noise of prongs going into an electrical outlet. Thirty seconds later, I felt the metal of the curling irons in my fingers begin to get warm.

TWO

Trust-fund money.

That's what I was born into. The interest my trust fund earns each day is more than most people make in a year. That doesn't make me special. It's not like I chose to be born into that kind of money.

I'm not that fond of trust-fund kids myself. Because they think I'm one of them, I have to endure those kids who think they *are* special because of where the womb dumped them. Occasionally, when stuck in their yacht clubs, private golf courses, private schools, etcetera, it's convenient to pretend I'm one of them.

I'm not.

Nor do I feel special.

For years I watched my father treat my younger brother like crap, disappointed that he didn't live up to the name they gave him: Bentley. That should tell you what my father is like. First, spending nearly three hundred grand for leather and steel and polished-walnut trim on one of only thirty-seven special editions of a Bentley ever produced. Second, being pretentious enough to give my brother the name of one of the world's most exclusive production cars. And third, heaping bitterness upon my brother all his life because he wasn't capable of living up to the name or being a showroom model that my parents could brag about to their friends.

I was in this gym because I did not want to be a trust-fund kid. This was my other identity. A place where I wasn't seen as special because of the trust fund, where my reputation depended on my guts and my willingness to work.

Until now, I'd thought I'd kept this identity a secret from everyone in my trust-fund life.

WHO SENT YOU TO THE DETECTIVE TO LOOK INTO THE HOSPITAL FILES?

The pain in my hands was growing unbearable. That was good. When I stopped feeling pain, it would mean the burns were third-degree, searing the nerve endings so badly that they stopped functioning.

I spoke, my voice sounding harsh and scratchy to me.

"You want answers?" I said. "Unplug the curling irons."

The pad jerked up and out of sight. The sound of the Converse shoes moving across the tiles again was a promise of relief that brought tears to my eyes.

I heard the click of the plug being pulled from the electrical outlet.

The pain in my hands didn't end immediately. I would have needed to run cool water over my hands to relieve the agony.

But it seemed like the heat was becoming less intense.

My tears ran down onto the top of my lip, and I licked away the salt.

The shoes shuffled back and reappeared outside the cubicle door. I memorized the scratch on the toe of the left shoe.

"If this is one of you two freak girls…" I said, thinking of Jo and Raven. And really, except for my brother Bentley, they were the only ones who knew I'd hired a detective to look into my father's past. And it wasn't Bentley on the other side of the door. The strides were too long.

So who could it be but the two of them, who knew what I'd done? I said, "This is a crappy test of loyalty. No way would anyone give up the use of their hands to prove they're on your team."

I heard the sound of another sheet being ripped from the pad, of the pencil scribbling on paper, and then the pad pushed over the top of the cubicle door and slid down again on the fishing line that held it.

GIVE ME THE NAMES OF THE GIRLS. THEN TELL ME WHY YOU WANT THE DETECTIVE LOOKING FOR THINGS AT THE HOSPITAL.

Naturally, I thought, if it was Jo and Raven doing this as a test, they would pretend not to know their own names. On the other hand, if it wasn't them, it was also a logical question from the unseen stranger in the Converse shoes.

"Amber Whitmore," I lied, thinking of a girl who sat in front of me in math class. And then of her friend. "Danielle McGowan. I hired the detective as a favor to them. I don't know what they expected to find out. I hoped it was something horrible. I don't like my father, and I was happy to help."

In case it wasn't Jo or Raven on the other side, the lie was a necessary protection for them. And for me. The only thing that wasn't a lie was the part about my father. I detested him.

Silence greeted my answer.

The pad of paper disappeared. Rip. Scratch. The pad appeared again on the end of the fishing line. Someone didn't even want me seeing his or her hands.

WHAT INFORMATION ARE YOU TRYING TO OBTAIN?

The truth was that I'd received an anonymous email informing me that my father had done something illegal at the hospital at the time of my brother's birth, and that it would help my brother if I found out what.

Not that I was going to reveal this. I'd been anticipating the question and had my answer ready.

"That," I said. "Right. They want me to harvest social-insurance numbers from the patient files."

Same routine of disappearing and returning pad of paper.

YOU SHOULD NOT HAVE LIED.

The second trip of the scuffling shoes had been a promise of relief. Now the shoes made a third trip to the electrical outlet, and this one filled me with dread.

"We want to sell the numbers to hackers in Russia!" I said in a half shout. I was ashamed of the panic in my voice. "I used my father's connections at the hospital to set it up!"

I held my breath, hoping to hear the shoes returning.

Instead, there was the click of the prong being inserted in the outlet. I felt the heat begin to build in the curling irons.

I threw my body as hard as I could against the duct tape that was holding me in place.

Incredibly, something gave.

It wasn't the tape. It was the pipe I'd been taped against, moving with a creaking sound.

Again I lunged forward. Twice. Three times. On the fourth time, there was a whoosh of water as the pipe gave way with such suddenness that I banged my head against the cubicle door.

It was a pain I didn't feel. Not when the insides of my fingers and my palms were screaming at the sun-hot pain inflicted by the curling irons.

With my hands between my knees, I jerked my wrists upward, and the cords snapped loose from the extension cord.

I swiveled to face the broken pipe and let the cold water rush down my arms and onto my hands. I held my wrists in the water for at least a minute, head turned to see if Converse would be back to kick open the cubicle door and attack.

Nothing.

The water pooled at my feet, and the agony of my hands disappeared.

Anger began to replace my fear.

I bounced my shoulder into the cubicle door. Then, when it didn't pop open, I gave it a full body slam and burst through, rolling onto the washroom floor, where the water from the burst pipe formed a wide and shallow pool.

I was completely soaked. With the curling irons still taped to my hands.

Before I could roll over and make it onto my knees, two pairs of shoes entered my vision. With them came two voices I recognized.

"So this is what a boys' bathroom looks like." This from Jo. "I have to say, Raven, I've always wondered."

THREE

First things first. This gym was Billy's pride. Billy's life. I needed to stop the gushing water. That would be as simple as reaching the plumbing shut-off valve.

I stood.

"Seriously," Jo said, looking from me to the busted cubicle door, back to me and the curling irons taped to my hands and then to the extension cord that led to an electrical outlet. "This is sick. Like, depraved sick."

That was more proof of what I already knew about her. Smart. Very smart. She'd followed the links and immediately come to the correct conclusion. Someone had been torturing me.

But then, maybe she'd been the one who came up with the idea. Because she was smart. Very smart.

"Who did this?" Jo asked. "Why?"

Jo was not tall. But thin, so she looked taller than she was. The type of thin that comes from living on the streets. She had Asian in her background, and something else, giving her skin a duskiness that was, well, as alluring as the rest of her. Long dark hair. Eyes that were intense brown.

I'd first met her at a park. Some dude had been trying to make life miserable for her, and I couldn't help but step in, more because I didn't like the dude's attitude and less because of trying to impress her. As a result, I didn't make a good impression on her. Then she had reappeared in my life at a chess match at my school. Bishops Prep. She and Raven had faked student ID cards and infiltrated the school, then blackmailed me into helping them.

It had been interesting, their approach, because they had blatantly used the fact that they were hot and knew it. I'd been forced to help them with a couple of their own projects that had barely ended well for them. Worse, from my perspective, they'd dragged Bentley into their messes.

In answer to Jo's question about the who and why of the curling irons, I shrugged. I didn't feel like speculating out loud to answer her questions. It seemed too convenient to me that both of them were here right at this time. For all I knew, one of them had been wearing the Converse shoes, and when they'd heard me break the pipes loose, they'd decided to switch roles, from interrogators to surprised visitors.

The more I thought about it, the more sense it made. That whole thing with the pad and paper. Silence would have been necessary, because speaking or whispering might have made it possible for me to identify them.

As Raven looked from the curling irons on my hands to the electrical outlet, her face showed the same thought process that Jo had followed. Difficult to decide which of the two was smarter. Or, frankly, better-looking. Raven had pale skin, like her ancestors had come from Ireland. She was tall, but not awkward or lanky. She had dark, layered hair down to her shoulders. Hence the name Raven. And she had attitude.

Raven said, "How bad are your hands?"

Maybe that was deliberate irony, based on the two of them being the ones who'd done this to me.

"I'm okay," I said. "It was only a threat."

If they'd set this up, I wasn't giving them the satisfaction of knowing that my fight adrenaline was wearing off and my palms and the insides of my fingers were giving me some serious pain.

I lifted my hands to my mouth and snapped my teeth on a loose strand of duct tape to pull it loose.

"Hey," Raven said. She reached out to help. "I can save you some time."

My first impulse was to yank myself out of her reach. I didn't need or want her help. Not in the mood I was in. With the water from the broken pipe flowing into the drain, an extra minute or two until I reached the shut-off valve wouldn't do any more damage to Billy's gym than had already been done.

Then I realized that if they were behind this and were now acting innocent, it would be smart to do some acting of my own. No sense in letting obvious anger on my part show that I was suspicious of them.

"Thanks," I said, putting a smile on my face that I didn't feel. I decided I was going to cooperate with them as long as it took to find out if and why they'd done this to me.

I held out my wrists.

Raven leaned over and began to unwind the duct tape. Raven. As in the girl who had once scaled the walls to the mansion where

Bentley and I lived and where Bentley and I suffered. Because of that, Raven knew I came from money. But I doubt she really understood how much money. The mansion, impressive as it was, was no indication of how deep the family fortune was.

With her this close, I could smell fresh shampoo. Like me, and like Jo, she'd wanted to take someone down. Hot-looking as both of them were, I'd not once allowed myself any boy-girl thoughts. The three of us had begun our limited relationship with them blackmailing me into helping them. I'd done what I needed to get them out of my life—until I'd called in a favor to get them to meet me tonight.

Raven finished pulling away the last of the duct tape.

I glanced at my palm and did my best not to let any emotion cross my face. Dime-sized blisters lined my fingers and dotted my palm, like my hand belonged to a gecko.

I used my right hand to free my left hand. I didn't open my left hand to look at what I knew I'd see, and I took a couple of quick steps to the exposed piping against the far wall. I turned the shut-off valve to stop the water flow from the broken pipe, and the pressure of the valve on my skin made me wince.

I made sure any expression of pain was gone as I turned back to them.

Jo pointed at the yellow sheets of paper that were now pulped in the water and sucked to the drain. She nudged one of the sheets out of the water, but it was as puddled as my skin would have been if the curling irons had been left on any longer.

Jo stepped closer to the toilet cubicle, where the pad was on the floor, away from the water flow and still dry, the fishing line still tied to the hole at the top.

She lifted it and studied the words written across the top page from the last of the scrawled statements put in front of me by Converse Person. She read it out loud to Raven. *"You should not have lied."*

Raven snorted. "In my life, it's telling the truth that gets me in trouble."

"No," Jo said. "That's what's on this page. These words: *You should not have lied.*"

Jo lifted the fishing line and let the pad dangle from the end of the nearly invisible nylon strand.

"Huh," she said.

She cocked her head. I could see her thoughts racing.

She walked to a neighboring cubicle, lifted the pad over the door and slid it down the other side, feeding out fishing line. Then she let go, and the pad slipped to the floor.

"Interesting," Jo said. She looked at me. "Care to explain?"

Before I could answer, a deep voice reached us from the interior of the gym.

"Vancouver Police," the voice said. "Canine Unit."

"Crap," Raven said. For Jo's benefit, she pointed toward the hallway that led to a back door. "Plan B." She looked at me. "Meet us at Denny's. One hour."

They were in motion before I could answer, abandoning me to the cops.

I followed. I had good enough reasons of my own not to be caught here in the gym by any type of authority.

FOUR

Just over an hour later we were settled in a booth at a Denny's restaurant on Davie Street. It was safe and anonymous.

Our salads had just arrived. I know. Salad.

"Why did the two of you break into the gym?" I asked.

I knew I'd locked the doors to work out in privacy.

"We didn't," Raven said. "The back door was open, with the lock broken. That's probably why the police were checking it out. But we would have broken in if we needed to. Security there is a joke. But we don't have to tell you that, do we?"

I wasn't going to let her change the subject.

"Then why," I said, "did you come looking for me? We had agreed to meet in the park."

"It's a little exposed out on the point," Raven said. "Too easy to get trapped."

"No reason to suspect a trap," I said. "All I wanted was a meeting."

I needed them to break into a house for me and steal a Picasso painting worth upward of a quarter million. They owed me, and I wasn't going to be afraid to let them know it.

"If it had anything to do with curling irons taped to your hands," Jo said, "then I'd say that's enough reason for us to suspect a trap."

"Except," I said, challenging them, "you couldn't know about the curling irons ahead of time. Right? And if you didn't know ahead of time, you still don't trust me."

Raven shrugged. "You know where Jo and I come from. Don't take it personally.

Besides, it's not all about you. We guessed if you had a reason to set up a meeting with us, then something bad enough was happening behind the scenes that we needed to take precautions."

Jo said, "We're always cautious. Otherwise we wouldn't be here right now. Anyone else back at the gym would have been flushed out by the Canine Unit to the cop in the alley at the back door."

That had been the obvious exit. Instead, Jo and Raven, with me behind them, had gone to the rooftop. Then they had checked the back alley from above. With the cop below, it meant going to the other side of the roof and jumping across a ten-foot gap to the building beside the gym. And then jumping to another rooftop and finally taking a fire escape down.

Always cautious. Like, maybe if they thought I had been setting a trap, they'd decided to break into the gym and pull the curling-iron trick to see if I'd give them up under any kind of pressure.

"Always cautious," I repeated. "That's why you followed me after we split up."

Jo studied me. "For a rich kid, I'm impressed. Not many would have noticed us tailing you. And if we suspected anything, we wouldn't be here."

"Why don't you trust me?" I asked.

"We don't trust anybody," Raven said. "Jo and I barely trust each other. That means we have some questions for you. These questions won't involve a curling iron."

They must have had a little girl talk while following me here.

"I'm not promising answers," I said.

"There was some pulped yellow paper in the drain at the gym," Raven said. "That means you'd already faced some questions before the one I saw on the paper. What did you lie about? How did paper person know you were lying about whatever the questions were?"

Both of them. Smart. Very smart.

And either the greatest actors of our time or truly innocent. I was on the bubble as to which was the correct of the two choices.

When I didn't answer, Jo said to me, "Don't pretend otherwise. Someone was interrogating you and using torture to get the answers. Someone who didn't want you to know his identity."

Or *her* identity, I wanted to say but kept silent.

Her hands were flat on the table as she continued, "Someone who forced you to answer enough questions to decide you were lying. At this point, I only know you at the surface level, but that's enough to know that if someone was trying to make you do something, anything at all, your first response would be to do the opposite, no matter how much it hurt you."

"Got to go with you on that one," Raven said to Jo. "He wouldn't have said a word until the curling irons heated up. And then only to buy some time to figure out how to get out of the situation. Let's see your hands."

"I'm a big boy," I said. "I don't need sympathy."

"And you're usually not an idiot," Raven said. "Jo and I aren't worried about your owie. The condition of your hands is significant to us for a much different reason. You show us your hands, or we walk."

These were not the kind of girls to make empty threats. Unfortunately, I needed them. So I put my wrists on the table and flipped my hands over.

The blisters were still growing. Tight bubbles of clear pus on my palms.

"Not good," Jo said to Raven. "Someone was serious about getting answers from him. But in his favor, the statement on the paper was that he lied. I'm willing to assume he didn't give us up. So let's give him a chance to tell us what favor he wants from us."

"Favor?" I said. "*Favor*? Both of you owe me. I set up the meeting to collect on a debt."

They *did* owe me. For how I had ensured Bentley would hack for them. For helping them deliver retribution. And now it was my turn.

To Jo, I said, "I want you to forge a painting so we can exchange it for the real thing."

To Raven, I said, "And once we have the real thing, you need to plant it for me."

FIVE

It was Tuesday evening, and my father, Dr. Winchester Wyatt, showed up for dinner, which was an unexpected and unpleasant surprise. Bentley and I rarely saw him, because he filled his calendar with work, bridge, golf and separate vacations to our other houses. He was, it appeared, content to be a self-indulgent loner.

Winchester surveyed the glossy and freshly servant-polished table and the five-course meal set up for my mother and Bentley and me and spoke in the cold, neutral voice he used whenever he and Bentley were in the same room.

"Bridge game canceled," Winchester announced. "You two and the midget leave anything decent for me to eat?"

By *the midget*, he meant Bentley. Here's some advice for you well-meaning people who will ask questions like, *What do I call a dwarf?*

Um, how about his or her first name?

And you should know that to someone like my brother, who was born with Laron syndrome, *midget* is a word that's as offensive as any racial slur. Winchester knew how offensive the word was and used it as often as possible.

As Winchester seated himself at the dining-room table, Bentley did what he always did when my father appeared. He left the room and retreated to his own bedroom, where he could assume a different persona at the computer. He truly was a computer genius, and that's where he escaped from the daily wounds of life resulting from how he appeared to those who did not know him and love him like I did.

Boxing for me, computer for him. See, the trust-fund life isn't as wonderful as you might think it is from the outside.

Bentley was born with Laron syndrome. It's a disorder resulting from an insensitivity to growth hormone. Bentley is very short and will remain that way all his life. He was born with a prominent forehead and a distinctly depressed nasal bridge, so there had been no mistaking how his life's destiny had been set for him.

It's a recessive-gene thing. Or, as Winchester would look at it, a faulty-gene thing. For a child to have Laron-type dwarfism, he or she needs to get the recessive gene from both parents. In other words, Bentley was proof to the world that not only did our mother carry the faulty gene, but so did the oh-so-perfect Winchester. And in his circles, everyone understood recessive genes and what that meant about Winchester.

It's not something a person gets tested for ahead of time. If so, I'm sure

Winchester would not have taken the chance of being a father, because if both parents had the recessive gene, it meant there was a one-in-four chance their child would be born with the dwarfism.

One in four.

Bentley and I haven't ever spoken about this, but that means I'm the one who dodged the genetic bullet. It could just as easily have been me who got both recessive genes when the game-winning sperm slammed into the egg to launch my blueprint for life.

And it could just as easily have been me to face the surgery inflicted on Bentley because of Winchester.

It involved sawing Bentley's thigh bones in half to insert titanium lengtheners. Um, *adjustable* lengtheners. The idea was that as soon as Bentley's muscles adapted and stretched, the titanium could be screwed a few notches longer. Like braces that gradually shape teeth.

It had happened a few years back, when Bentley was still doing everything possible to earn any kind of love from Winchester he could. Bentley had put on a brave, it-doesn't-hurt kind of face so Winchester wouldn't be disappointed. But I'd seen the tears. Bentley rocking as he clutched his ribs with both arms to try to contain the pain. And the heartache, knowing he'd never be good enough for Winchester.

Bentley was my brother, and I would die for him if that meant saving his life. I'd long since learned, however, that Winchester took great satisfaction whenever I tried to defend Bentley from his attacks, because it gave him a chance to degrade Bentley even more. My father was to all appearances a perfect man. It didn't take Bentley's genius to realize that to Winchester, Bentley was an imperfection that let the world know Dr. Winchester Wyatt had spoiled seed.

*　*　*

"Food?" my father asked upon entering the dining room.

"Ring the maid for leftovers," my mother said. And she left the room.

This was their usual way of communicating. By *not* communicating. They had separate bedrooms and did not hide the fact that any love they'd once shared had not only disappeared, but also had been replaced by cold indifference to one another.

"Just you and me then," Winchester said to me. "How was school?"

He looked at the way I was holding my fork.

"Something happen to your hand?" he asked.

I opened my hand and showed him the blisters that were so painful they were turning my hands into claws. He was a brilliant man, and it would be futile to try to hide them from him.

"Grabbed a Bunsen burner that I thought was cold," I said. I tried to make a joke. "It got me out of chemistry class at least."

"Don't miss too much class," Winchester said. "No mark lower than a ninety-seven. At least one of my sons should be able to make our family proud."

Some fathers might have shown concern about whether I was getting proper treatment for the burns.

I pushed away from the table and left in silence. He was my father, and I'd done my best not to hate him. But over the last few years, I'd been losing that battle, so all I could do was say as little as possible when I was in his presence.

I intended to stop by Bentley's room and update him on the detective and our plans to find out why the anonymous email had been sent to us.

As soon as possible after that, I would escape the house and lead my other life. The life that was real because no one in it knew that I had been born into the Croft fortune.

SIX

When I reached Bentley's suite of rooms, I knew exactly where to look for him. On a cushion on a window seat in a far alcove.

The irony of his living situation wasn't lost on either of us, given the contrast between his size and the size of his living quarters. His bedroom was double the size of most living rooms. One door led to a bathroom, with tub, steam shower and separate shower, that was bigger than most bedrooms. On the far side of the bedroom, a wide opening led to a den area with a couch and a monstrous wide-screen television. Beyond that, a room for his computers and then a small library with the window alcove that overlooked the grounds.

My own living quarters mirrored his, but where he'd made a library, I had chosen to set up a small workout area with weights and treadmills. Don't think for a moment that we had these luxuries because Winchester wanted us to enjoy life. Not a chance. He wanted to be able to parade guests through the mansion and show them that he was the type of man who spared nothing for his family.

"Hey," Bentley said.

"Hey," I said. No point in any encouraging words, like, *Yeah, Dad must be in a bad mood—he didn't really mean what he said*. First, it would have been laughable to call Winchester by any other name than Winchester. He wasn't a dad. He was a biological father. Second, Bentley and I both knew that Winchester always meant what he said when he threw out barbed words. And third, we'd been through that conversation endlessly during our younger years, with Bentley crying and me raging, until we'd finally accepted that it wouldn't change, and then we'd come to a more important understanding: we weren't going to blame ourselves for Winchester's treating us the way he did. And, no surprise, that made us tight as brothers.

"Tell me about your hands," Bentley said. He was looking out the window at the rich greens of the trees and lawn against the backdrop of the mountains. Billion-dollar view. Still didn't make up for a biological father who scorned us as failures.

"Thought you'd notice," I said. "It was a pair of curling irons."

Bentley swung his legs toward me, and his feet hung over the edge of the window seat.

There had been a time when his feet wouldn't even reach the edge. Then Winchester had arranged for Bentley to have an artificial growth spurt compliments of Frankenstein surgery. It didn't matter to Winchester that following the surgery Bentley would be in agony for months. What did matter to Winchester was an attempt for Bentley to look normal. As I mentioned, Winchester was supposed to spawn manly football-hero type boys, not boys with Laron-type dwarfism.

"Curling irons?" Bentley said. Around me, he was different than he was around other people. He could be gentle and vulnerable.

"Curling irons." In a flat voice, I recounted it for him, including my suspicions about Jo and Raven.

"Bro," he said, "I tend to trust them."

He caught my look. "I know what you're thinking, but it's not because they are hot, and believe me, I'm aware they're hot. And it's not because they're cool around me."

Which meant they didn't pity him. Nor did they pretend he was built normally. It was impossible not to notice his size.

"I think they share some kind of honor code," Bentley said. "Them against the world. Lie to authorities, but not to those the authorities are trying to crush."

"If not them," I said, "who? Schmedley has reported nothing back to me."

Schmedley wasn't the guy's real name—we called him that because he dressed sloppy and had a sloppy haircut and sloppy gut. It was Vince Crowther. He was a former Vancouver cop, now set up as a private investigator. He'd worked for the family of a kid we knew at school. And after receiving the email with the accusation against Winchester, I'd been happy to hire him to look into it, trusting him because of his reputation and not his looks.

"But," Bentley said, "what if all the poking around Schmedley has done actually knocked something loose?"

I snorted. "Like, Winchester is suddenly scared and did that to me himself?"

For a second I considered it. But Winchester wouldn't do his own dirty work.

"Not his style," Bentley confirmed, as if he was reading my mind. "Would he send someone after you?"

"Look," I said. "That person would have to know how to find me. Remember, at the gym I have my secret identity."

I paced a few steps and came back. "It might prove, though, that there is some truth to what's in the email. I think you've been right all along. The key is Dr. Evans, the chief of staff. He's the one who has handled discipline hearings at the hospital for years. We're going to have to go down that road."

"Jo and Raven on board?"

"Do they have a choice? Remember, we helped them when they needed it."

"Tomorrow?"

"Tomorrow," I said. "Jo and Raven will be there to help me."

My job was Evans and I needed them for that. I didn't think it was a good plan, but it was the best that Bentley and I had been able to come up with.

Bentley's job was computer stuff. "Any success on your end?" I asked. He lifted his right fist, like it was a salute. On his wrist was a tattoo. It was the shape of an elongated eight, on its side. The symbol for infinity.

I smiled. "All those possibilities."

That's one of the things I loved about Bentley. He believed that life was filled with endless possibilities. And opportunities. My love for him was reflected in that same tattoo on my right shoulder blade.

"Nothing yet on the hospital computers," he said, then dropped his wrist. "I got in again and roamed around, but zilch to point us to anything Winchester's done wrong."

"No worries," I said. "That's why we hired the detective."

Bentley and I had agreed I should do it as the inner-city boxer kid, my identity away from the mansion. Better protection for us. So I had worn grungy clothes when I'd visited the detective. I'd paid him in crumpled bills. I'd told him my name was Jace Sanders, the name I used at the gym as a boxer. No way did Bentley and I want Schmedley knowing we were hiring him to investigate our own father, a high-society darling of the local media.

"What about the email that started all this?" I asked Bentley. "Any luck there?"

"Yeah," he said, voice flat. "Success."

Something about Bentley's tone of voice sounded like alarm bells.

"Jace," he said. "I was able to trace the email to the IP address. It came from the computer in her office."

"Her?"

"Mother. Margaret Croft."

SEVEN

If you were found dead with a three-inch-long piece of unchewed meat blocking your windpipe, chances are someone might suspect it was murder. Especially if Soviet spies were chasing you.

That's what I was thinking about the next morning at school while I watched an arrogant smile cross the face of my chess opponent, a seventeen-year-old who believed he was the center of the universe because he'd been plopped into the crib somewhere in the depths of a mansion within hours of his birth.

His name was Jed Murgoyd. Tall, braces, wire-rim glasses and an already developed set of wrinkles around his mouth from constantly pursing it in disapproval at the world. He thought he was a chess expert because he understood terms like Qg3 and Nd5, algebraic notation for chess moves. He also thought he was an expert because he'd thrown a Marshall Defense at me in what at this point was an unfolding attempt to mimic a classic 1925 game between Frank James Marshall and Alexander Alekhine. As if I couldn't recognize it.

We were hunched on opposite sides of a chess board in a cafeteria called Lounge A in Bishops Prep High School— a frequent scene in my alternate but artificial life.

This was the kind of school where the hallways were always hushed in anticipation of yet another graduate somewhere in the country sending word of yet another coronation. Senator. CEO of a major corporation. Prime minister. Those kinds of achievements, all adding yet another photo to yet another hallway so that the rest of us could walk beneath their gazes with the unspoken promise that yes, we too would honor the school's tradition.

Murgoyd and I had reached move fourteen on the board. I'd just gone Qe3 from Qd2—sent my queen from the second row forward and the square fourth from the left to the third row forward and fifth from the left—a back-to-back move that should have alerted him that I was replicating Alekhine's strategy. Inching forward like that on the surface showed fear, especially given Alekhine's reputation for a fierce and imaginative attacking style.

Now I had to sit and watch the permutations cross Murgoyd's face. Was he going to pretend to take the bait and follow in Marshall's footsteps by attacking with bishop to c6? Or would he actually do something original in his life?

Which gave me time. Too much time. To wonder about who had been wearing the white Converse shoes and why Raven and Jo had shown up at the gym and how the cops had arrived so quickly and what they had been expecting.

Much more pleasant to think about the inglorious end of Alexander Alekhine, which was officially blamed on a heart attack even after the autopsy strongly implied that someone had shoved steak down his throat. But hey, those were the Russians, and that was the Cold War. Not nice and civilized like now, when people taped curling irons to your hands.

It hurt just to twitch my fingers. That was another thing I didn't want to think about. What it would be like later in the day to form fists inside boxing gloves and repeatedly slam a heavy bag for half an hour.

Finally, Murgoyd made his move. Bishop to c6. Shocker. A diagonal move that left his king slightly exposed.

I pretended to think. The best move would have been to switch castle and king o-o-o, and he would have probably followed suit on the opposite end of the board, but a shorter distance o-o.

Instead, I messed with Murgoyd by moving Qf4, putting him in a position of taking my unprotected queen.

There should have been gasps around me—if the spectators were knowledgeable about chess. My chess games usually drew the dweeb crowd, most of them posers following the school's current fashion of celebrating intellect. The posing stopped at the end of the school day, because girls never choose the smart ones, but during school hours it impressed the teachers, and Bishops Prep was the kind of school where that actually mattered.

Murgoyd, at least, wasn't a poser, and he muttered, not believing my stupidity. And because I wasn't known as a stupid player, this made him doubly suspicious. Was I throwing a Marshall move right back at him? Frank James Marshall had become legendary for his "swindle" moves—using tricks that seemed like magic to turn games around.

The dweebs around us leaned in for a better look, only because they had been clued in by Murgoyd's muttering and were trying to understand what was unusual about my chess move.

It was exactly what I needed. At this moment, at the far end of the lounge, Jo was nudging open Jed Murgoyd's backpack. She was wearing one of our school's boy uniforms and had performed the anatomically impossible feat of taking the curves out of her body to become almost invisible as a boy.

I knew she was digging out Murgoyd's keys and needed less than sixty seconds to make an impression of them.

The reason was simple, really. She believed she needed to, so that Raven could steal a painting from Murgoyd's father and Jo could then forge it.

Did I care that I was in danger of losing a chess game because of it? Yes, I did care.

If he won, I'd have to put up with Murgoyd's haughty superiority until a rematch.

So I dug in and found a way to kick Murgoyd's butt, taking petty satisfaction when he was forced to topple his king. Murgoyd had no idea what had happened to his backpack. But then, neither did Jo. Because the key I'd helped her steal was one I'd planted there ahead of time.

EIGHT

Raven stood on the sidewalk across from the Greyhound bus station, where I had just pulled up. The top was down on the Mustang convertible so that I could talk to her without rolling down the passenger window. I was not in a great mood. Inching through downtown traffic in Vancouver will do that to a person, even when the sun is shining. It didn't help my mood that my hands were scabbing from blisters that had broken while I was working the heavy bag in the gym the evening before.

"This cloak-and-dagger stuff is getting old," I told her. Her instructions had been to head toward Chinatown for our 11:00 AM meeting. She had then called my cell five minutes before eleven to give me the final destination, so I wouldn't know ahead of time where she would be waiting. Obviously, she still suspected I would try to set up some kind of trap. Given my own plans, she had no idea how right she was not to trust me.

"Get used to it," she said. Then walked around to my side of the car and opened the door. "I'm driving."

Behind us, a woman in a Toyota Prius honked.

Raven flipped her the bird.

The woman honked again.

"Excuse me," Raven said. "I'll have this handled by the time you get in the passenger seat."

I didn't like someone telling me what to do. But it would feel good not to have to grip the steering wheel. And it would suit my purpose for Raven to believe she was in control. Besides, she was a car thief. I could trust her ability to drive.

I stepped out of the Mustang while Raven strolled to the Prius to have a chat with the woman behind us. To my right were the bus terminal and the railway station. Plenty of pedestrians. And plenty of homeless people. Beautiful weather for an aimless morning.

As I walked around the hood of the Mustang, I saw Raven leaning into the driver's window of the Prius. The Mustang was jet black. The Prius, appropriately, a dull green.

Raven returned to the Mustang and slid into the driver's seat.

"Nice chat?" I said. As far as I could tell, no punches had been thrown.

"I pointed out that her smug self-righteousness at driving a Prius was misplaced. That studies have shown a gas-guzzling Tahoe SUV has a smaller carbon footprint than her I'm-better-than-the-rest-of-the-world status symbol. People don't put together what it takes to have all those batteries for a Prius. I say ride a bike or take the bus."

"Oh," I said. "That's nice."

Raven patted the steering wheel. "Slumming it, are we?"

The convertible was less than two weeks old. But the last car she'd seen me in was a Lamborghini.

"Borrowed it," I said. "From a girl at school."

I saw a slight tensing of her jaw muscles. I knew she didn't like Bishops Prep and the pretentiousness there. It upset her that a daddy would give his teenage daughter a brand-new Mustang. It was an attitude I understood. And shared.

"Just took a flash of your pearly whites, did it?" Raven asked. "A flex or two of your biceps and she tossed you the keys?"

"Shallow gender stereotyping doesn't suit you," I said. "By suggesting I am just a pretty face and that she cares only for my body, you belittle her and me."

"Exactly," Raven said. And gunned the Mustang, swerving hard. The rear tires squealed and slid across the asphalt, and a split second later we were facing the opposite direction, accelerating hard.

Two seconds later, she stomped on the brake for the red light at the intersection.

"You know," I said, aware of people staring at us, "the entire point of my borrowing someone else's car was to be inconspicuous. Perhaps you don't understand the definition of that word."

I spoke slowly, breaking it down to syllables. "In. Con. Spic. U. Ous."

"And perhaps you don't understand how dangerous I am when I'm in a bad mood," Raven said. "This whole break-in thing is Mickey Mouse. It's not like we're hitting some skid-row house with bars across the windows. A place like this, on the coastline, it's going to run in the millions. We're talking sophisticated security.

Video, silent alarm, maybe even rent-a-cop patrols. I have no idea of the layout or what we're up against. And I'm supposed to trust that you've got all the angles covered? A trust-fund kid who trades down from a Lamborghini to a Mustang and whose most difficult decisions in life are whether to ring the maid for tea or coffee with breakfast?"

I should have been offended by her insults. But I took her anger as a good sign. It meant she was distracted. I needed her distracted. If she stayed distracted, she wouldn't see the scam I was pulling on her.

"Got the breakfast decision covered," I said. "Usually Earl Grey tea. And freshly squeezed orange juice."

The light turned green. She floored the Mustang and expertly fought the skid, then zipped in and out of the traffic.

I hid my smile. Yup. An angry person was easier to fool than one who was thinking.

NINE

The drive took a little over half an hour. From the grittiness of the east end of downtown Vancouver, we traveled through layers of wealth reflected by buildings and storefronts that went from tattoo parlors and pawnshops to fur-coat storage and jewelry stores, from motels to high-rise luxury hotels. The end of downtown threw us into Stanley Park, onto the Lions Gate Bridge, then past the immaculate lawns and pruned hedges and trees of West Vancouver. We followed the Trans-Canada Highway until it abandoned us for the ferry terminal at Horseshoe Bay. We jumped onto Highway 99—the Sea to Sky Highway—to follow the coastline north, a route familiar to me because of endless trips during my childhood.

My phone's turn-by-turn directions were the only sounds in the car.

Deep-green, tree-covered coastal mountains to our right. Flashes of the waters of the strait to our left. Then an exit right and a left-hand turn onto the overpass and into a gated community, well screened from the highway noise by trees and walls.

I opened the glove compartment and pulled out a garage-door opener. I pointed it at the gate and clicked. The gate swung open.

"She lives in this community too?" Raven said, referring to the girl she believed had loaned me the car.

I shrugged, knowing my insolence would stoke Raven's anger. "The millionaire-billionaire community is not large."

Raven gave me a deadpan glance that said she wasn't impressed. She drove us around the curves, past the high hedges and to where the road dead-ended at a house high enough to be visible over the walls that guarded it.

"Go up the driveway and park," I said, "like we are expected friends."

"I don't need that kind of help from you," she snarled. "What I need to know is which of the keys works."

At Bishops Prep, when Jo had made impressions of the keys in Murgoyd's backpack during the chess game, she'd had no choice but to take impressions of all seven keys before returning them to his backpack. Two were obviously car keys, so that left us with five.

"It will be easy to figure out. Try them one by one and see which fits."

"Remind me again how you know the security code?" she said.

"Nope," I said. "I need to protect my source."

"I don't like this."

"I'm in just as much danger as you are," I said. "You'll have to trust me. Wear the ballcap in the trunk and keep your head down. The video cameras won't be able to identify you."

"I don't—"

"I know. You don't trust me. Too bad. I'm going to sit in the car," I said. "You know, as lookout."

"First," she said, "call again. I want to hear the phone ringing."

This was a realistic request. I'd assured her that I'd been at this house many times. That there was a phone near the front entrance.

I pulled out my cell. An unanswered phone meant no one was home. I dialed the number, confident that when she reached the door, she'd hear the phone.

With the cell phone to my ear, I smiled sweetly at Raven. "Go ahead. And don't forget the painting. It's in the trunk."

"Idiot," she said.

Such venom.

She popped the trunk and took out a small backpack. The painting wasn't large.

It was the forgery I had asked Jo to do for me.

I was impressed at her acting. She flounced up the driveway with the backpack slung over her shoulder on one strap, like she was one of the privileged, one of the elite, one of the few.

She disappeared around a corner of the hedge.

I leaned back and lifted my face to the sun. The warmth felt good.

I closed my eyes briefly but opened them again as I heard tires on the driveway and the idling of a car. I glanced in the rearview mirror.

A sentry car.

It belonged to the neighborhood security force of hired wannabe cops.

I got out of the Mustang. I stretched with pretended casualness. It was definitely pretended. I had to get rid of this guy quickly.

I wandered to the driver's side of his vehicle, a Ford Fusion with a decal of a shield on the side.

"Freddy," I said to the driver. "Glad to be off the night shift?"

He was balding and middle-aged.

"Darn straight," he said. "You doing okay?"

"Great," I said. "Sorry that I didn't register the Mustang with the checklist at the gate. It's just a rental. I'm here to pick something up, so I sent my friend inside in case you showed up wondering who was here. And sure enough, it took you less than a minute. Good work."

"Gave me something to do," he said.

What it did, I knew, was take him away from watching classic-football-game reruns in the guard shack down by the golf course.

I felt the seconds ticking by. If Raven came back out, she'd freak. And I'd have some explaining to do.

"Well," I said, "now you know the Mustang belongs here, we're cool, right? I guess I'll head inside and join my friend."

Freddy saluted me and put the vehicle in reverse. He eased out of the driveway and then headed back to his reruns. There was nothing to concern him. I was parked in front of my own house. I'd gone through this all for Raven's benefit.

Thirty seconds later, Raven made it back outside, carrying the backpack.

"All good?" I said.

"Switch made," she said. "Now let's get out of here. That was so easy it's making me nervous."

TEN

How you want to wake up is drowsy, in clean, comfortable sheets, with stripes of sunlight on your face from the slats of the blinds on a bedroom window. Not to the punched-in-the-brain jolt of ammonium carbonate crystals mixed with water.

Yeah. Smelling salts. In boxing, that jolt is a powerful clue that in the previous sixty seconds or so, you made an error of such proportions that someone rang your bell like the hunchback of Notre Dame.

Some athletes—like hockey players— use the salts specifically to get that whoosh of clarity at exhaustion points in a game. It's a sensation slightly less violent than a slap in the face and gives an adrenaline rush of clarity and focus.

Me? I'd prefer the slap in the face. The sting of ammonia gas up the nostrils is about as pleasant as vomiting. It triggers an inhalation reflex that snaps you back into the present world and makes your entire nervous system surge with activity.

It also brings your eyes back into focus. Which meant that following an indeterminate period of unconsciousness after taking a hard downward punch across the top of my right cheekbone, I had the questionable pleasure of seeing Billy's face right above mine as he leaned over my body in concern.

"Hey, stupid," he said. "Welcome back."

Billy's face would never get lost in a crowd. He was bald and fifty. Or maybe bald and seventy. It was a prematurely old face with the clichéd pug nose of a boxer who had cycled a half dozen times through broken, healed and rebroken.

"Hello, beautiful," I said. "Give me a kiss."

"Aack." He pushed away from me, giving me space to sit.

I could replay it now. Ducking and weaving, effortlessly slipping beneath and around the heavy punches of my sparring partner, someone six inches taller, forty pounds heavier and a jar of molasses slower than me.

What had happened was I'd noticed a guy outside the ring, at the speed bag, wearing white Converse leather shoes. A guy in a shiny blue tracksuit, maybe mid-twenties, reddish hair. I'd realized—too late—that my sparring partner was throwing in a big slow bomb of a punch that even a granny in a walker could avoid. And I'd gone down hard.

Hence the smelling salts and Billy's concern.

Brutus, my sparring partner, was grinning at me with the blackened teeth of someone still wearing his mouthguard.

Mine was gone. Billy, of course, would have reached in and popped it out as he checked to make sure my tongue hadn't fallen back into my throat.

Some trainers wore rubber surgeon's gloves before touching saliva. Not old-school Billy.

"Next time, dude," I told Brutus.

He laughed and punched his hands together in anticipation, the smack of his massive boxing gloves echoing in the ring.

I waved him away, signaling that I was done. It wasn't that I didn't want to go back into the ring and continue sparring with Brutus, but that I wanted to track down the red-haired Converse-shoe guy. What were the odds that two pairs of white leather shoes like that had the same scratch across the toe?

Billy followed me to a quiet corner of the gym.

"Never thought in a million years that guy could tag you," Billy said. It wasn't meant to bolster my spirits. Billy wasn't that type of fake motivator. He called it as he saw it. "You sure you're ready for Saturday's fight?"

"I'm ready," I said. "Trust me—it was a freak thing."

He nodded. "Okay then. Why not? It's been a freak week."

"You mean the break-in," I said. "And you're sure nothing was taken?"

I was glad my hands were taped up to hide the barely healing blisters. I'd lied to Billy about the night with the curling irons. I'd told him I'd locked up and was gone before the cops showed up. If I hadn't lied, there would have been the obvious questions, like, *Why would someone want to torture you with curling irons duct-taped to your hands?*

Just as dangerous, however, would have been questions about my identity. To Billy, I was Jace Sanders, a kid from an inner-city high school, trying to rise above a bad family life. To the cops, however, it would have taken about three minutes to figure out that Jace Sanders didn't exist and that my driver's license said *Jace Wyatt*. Then Billy would have found out that I lived behind the high stone walls of the exclusively rich, pretending that every punch I threw was a punch directly into my father's face.

So yes, I felt bad about the ongoing lie. I wouldn't pretend it was justified, because a lie is a lie. But I wouldn't apologize for it either. That was part of living a double life.

"Nothing stolen," he confirmed. "That's part of what makes it freaky. And if it wasn't weird enough already, why would they vandalize the locker room and break a water pipe? To add to the freakiness, out of nowhere, the plumbers tell me that somebody covered the bill. Go figure."

"Go figure," I said. The repairs had cost nearly a grand. I knew that kind of money would hurt Billy. And, sadly, it was mere pocket change from my other life.

"Hey," I said. "Looked like someone new in the gym. Red-haired guy, blue tracksuit. He any good?"

"I guess we'll find out," Billy said. "He's looking for a sparring partner. Tell me when you're ready to step into the ring with him."

Billy snorted again. "And that's another weird thing. He's the same guy who complained his shoes were gone when he came in the morning after the break-in. Said maybe he'd have to put a lock on his locker if this was the kind of place I ran. But lo and behold, I walk once around the gym and find the shoes tossed into a corner by the heavy bag. Explain *that*."

So Tracksuit Guy was just another gym rat. Whoever had tortured me had borrowed Tracksuit Guy's shoes. Which meant I was no closer to knowing who had been on the other side of the door, dropping notes by fishing line.

When I looked at Billy, I spoke the truth.

"Explain it, Billy?" I said. "I wish I could."

ELEVEN

"The way it's going to work," Raven said to me later that night, "is that when I reach the window, I'll drop some rope from my backpack. You attach it to your climbing belt. Once I've secured the top end, I'll give two sharp tugs. That's when you start jugging."

"Jugging?"

"Climbing the wall. For an athlete like you, that shouldn't be a problem."

It was just after midnight. She and I stood with Jo in the shadows of some bushes at the hospital building where my father worked. Three stories above us was a window to the office of the chief of staff, Dr. Evans. I'd made sure to unlatch the window earlier that day. Because I was the son of the world-famous neurosurgeon Dr. Winchester Wyatt, most of the staff and other physicians were accustomed to seeing me in the hallway near his office. Opening the latch had not been a problem.

But climbing the wall? That was definitely a problem.

"Last we discussed this, you were going solo," I said.

"Change of plans," Raven said. "Jo is here to stand guard, so that means you can climb and bring down the risk factor for me. If I go up alone, all you're risking is whether you can outrun a cop or security guard while I'm stuck on the wall. With you on the wall with me and we get caught, all we need to do is ditch the painting and pretend it was some kind of urban-climbing stunt dare. Your father is the big cheese around here. At worst, we get a slap on the wrist and a kids-will-be-kids kind of lecture."

There was a lot of truth in what she said. I could probably burn down part of the hospital and not even have to stand in front of a judge. But not because of my father. Given the scorn in her voice about my father's big-cheese status, I was glad Raven didn't know that my mother had been Margaret Croft before becoming Mrs. Margaret Wyatt. Because then Raven might have put together the fact that the Croft name on this hospital wing came from my mother's family, just like most of the wealth that was drowning me slowly. Neurosurgeons made decent money, but it took third-generation forest-and-mining wealth to possess Bentleys and Lamborghinis and private jets and mansions scattered around the world. My father had married wisely, trading his status as an up-and-coming surgeon with a handsome face and charming smile for the gilded cage that he craved.

"I don't like changes of plan," I said. I also didn't like Raven's sullen attitude. It was like she'd caught me kicking a kitten and hated me for it. "What happened to the let's-be-a-team attitude you liked so much when each of you needed my help?"

Actually, what I didn't like was the thought of wall walking. I was afraid of heights.

"Too bad," Raven said. "Jo came up with the idea, I voted in favor, and that makes it a two-thirds majority. You're not afraid, are you?"

I could feel sweat on my palms, stinging the broken blisters. I was really afraid of heights. Even seeing a movie scene shot at the top of a building gave me the sweats.

"One small problem," I said. "I forgot my climbing belt. Left it in the Himalayas during my last climb. A little hill called Everest."

"Jo?" Raven said.

Jo slipped out of the shoulder straps of her backpack. She reached in, pulled out a belt and tossed it to me.

"That should fit," she said. Same sullen attitude. It was starting to irritate me. I'd never kicked a kitten, and I didn't intend to.

Raven worked her own backpack loose and pulled out a corded rope. In the dimness, I could see large clip-like objects attached to the rope.

"These are Jumars," she said.

"Right. Jumars."

"Don't get smart-ass with me. They are the best ascenders money can buy. I'm going to go up on a free climb, but I don't think it's something you should try. The Jumars will slide upward freely and hold when you pull down. You'll have one for each hand. I've got a locking mechanism that will make sure your end of the rope follows you up so that it serves as a safety harness in case you're stupid enough to let go of the Jumars."

"Raven?" Jo said.

"Yeah."

"Give him the gloves, okay? I know it won't break your heart if those blisters hurt him, but if he lets go, it's going to be a pain for all of us."

So now I was learning that Raven *liked* that my blisters hurt?

"Of course," Raven said in a flat voice. She tossed me a pair of thick leather gloves.

It wasn't too late to turn around. But anger was a powerful motivator. Enough to overcome my fear.

"Wonderful," I told Raven. "Can't tell you how much I'm looking forward to this."

TWELVE

The best boxing match—I mean ever—
was Muhammad Ali against George
Foreman. Zaire, 1974. It's called "The
Rumble in the Jungle."

I watch it twice a month, pulling it up
from video archives. Foreman went into
the fight as a twenty-four-year-old heavy-
weight who had demolished opponents
with his punching power and sheer size
and physical dominance. Ali had speed
and boxing skills but was eight years
older than Foreman and considered a
worn-out underdog.

But Ali had a secret plan. He called it
the rope-a-dope. When the second round

began, Ali began leaning on the ropes, covering up. Foreman threw tremendous punches, but Ali deflected them away from his head and fired occasional jabs that were straight punches to Foreman's face.

In clinches, Ali leaned on Foreman, to make the bigger man support Ali's weight, and taunted him, telling him to throw more punches. Enraged, Foreman threw them harder and harder.

In the seventh round, seemingly beaten, Ali held Foreman in yet another clinch and whispered into Foreman's ear, "That all you got, George?"

That's when the bigger, stronger and favored fighter realized the fight wasn't what he thought it was. His first premonition, his first tremor of fear. In the eighth round, all those wild angry punches took their toll, and Foreman started losing strength.

It gives me an adrenaline rush to watch it in slow motion, the five-punch combination that Ali threw after a series of right hooks as Foreman tried to pin Ali against the ropes. Five punches, rapid-fire, precision missiles ending in a left hook that brought Foreman's head up into a vulnerable position, followed by a hard right from Ali that sent Foreman to the canvas, the knockout punch that ended the fight.

I've counted the punches that Ali took during those eight rounds. Hundreds. Thunderous blows from the world's most powerful puncher. Blows to Ali's sides. To his kidneys. To Ali's forearms. To Ali's biceps. Blows that bounced off his skull. Ali's response will always echo for me. *That all you got, George?*

I'd been living in a household dominated by a man the entire world believed to be a hero, and I'd seen what the world hadn't seen. I'd endured it since I was a boy. Blow after blow—not physical, but worse: blows of scorn and insults. Now here I was, climbing a rope on the side of a hospital building, trying to put in place a combination of counterblows to bring him down.

Yeah, I was scared of gravity. But I kept whispering to myself, That all you got?

Halfway up the wall I realized I was winning the fight against my fear. The process just took determination and a willingness to believe that if you hung in there—ha! Nice pun, given the rope that dangled three stories down the side of the hospital in the dark night—you'd win in the end.

I'd pull on the Jumar with my left hand, trusting that the mechanism would lock and hold. With my right hand, I'd slide the other Jumar up as high as I could. Then I'd pull down on the right Jumar, locking it in place, and slide the left Jumar up.

The effort didn't hurt my biceps or forearms. My boxing workouts had left me with plenty of strength. But alternating the weight of my body from my left hand to my right and back to my left was tearing at the broken and crusted blisters. Without the leather gloves, it would have been unbearable.

Pain I could deal with. Just like Ali. You took the shots until you were ready to fire them back in return.

The climb took ten minutes.

Raven had already opened the window to Dr. Evans's office, and I pulled myself through, ready to throw the first in a combination of punches.

"Slack job you have," I told Raven. "Climbing's nothing."

She was standing in the total darkness with a tiny flashlight to give us the light we needed.

"Not when someone's gone up with no rope and put one in place for you." I didn't hear a smile in her voice. "Let's get this done."

No time to worry about her attitude.

"All we do," I said, "is put the painting on his desk."

She pulled it out of her backpack. A small Picasso portrait. It was one of his early works. It was a distorted portrait of a woman, who complained to Picasso when it was finished that it didn't look like her at all. His tart reply was that someday it would. Historians called it Cubist, and I didn't care why. All I knew was how much it was worth and that every time Dr. Evans had been at our oceanside vacation property, he'd spent a lot of time looking at it with open lust.

The rest would depend on his reaction to finding it.

"What about the video?" Raven asked.

"Of course," I said.

Want to spy on people? Just google *spy video gadgets*, and you'll find a dozen ways that video cams are disguised. Ballcap visors, rocks, wall clocks, wristwatches.

I'd chosen a ballpoint cam. It was an expensive-looking ballpoint pen capable of recording color video and sound for thirty-two hours.

Raven handed three of them to me from her backpack. I'd given them to her earlier, when I'd thought she would be climbing the wall alone. Expense wasn't an issue for me. I doubted Dr. Evans would notice them in a fancy cuplike penholder he kept on a shelf. If, for some reason, he grabbed one to write with, that left a couple of others in place. And the pen would write, if necessary.

I touched the button on each of the pens to start the recording, then set them in the cup on the shelf in such a way that they would clearly capture the painting on Dr. Evans's desk when the sunlight came in through the window.

What Raven didn't know was that earlier in the day, when I'd wandered into Dr. Evans's office to open the window latch, I'd placed a fourth pen there to record her breaking into the office.

Lack of trust was a two-way game.

THIRTEEN

At the window, as we prepared to climb back down, Raven said, "When you get to the bottom, unhook the rope from your climbing belt and give two tugs. I'll know you're free. Then step away with Jo, because after a ten-count, I'll be throwing the rope down from the top, and I don't want to hit her. The hook at the end looks small, but at the speed it will be coming down, it's going to be dangerous."

I tried to lighten the mood. "Not worried about hitting me?"

Her answer was a grunt.

I wasn't successful in fighting a quick surge of temper. "What's with the attitude?"

I said. "You and Jo are treating me like dog poop to scrape off a shoe."

"We owed you this help, and you're getting it," Raven said. "Why should you care what attitude comes with it? But if you want to know, we're seriously not happy about the blackmail thing and how you threatened to turn us in to the authorities if we didn't help."

"Didn't say I cared," I snapped back. "It was just an observation."

"Then keep it to yourself. When we're on the ground, that's the last you'll see of us. Our debt to you will be paid, and you can go back to preppie heaven."

"Sounds like a good plan to me," I said. Especially because there was a better than fifty-fifty chance it had been the two of them torturing me with curling irons.

Raven had removed the Jumars and replaced them with belay devices. These were simple hand brakes with the rope threaded through them to slow my descent. I pulled on the leather gloves and gritted my teeth in anticipation of the pain. I lowered myself over the windowsill and began to slowly slide down the rope, using the belay devices as Raven had instructed to brake myself against gravity.

It was far easier going down than up.

I landed softly a few minutes later.

"Top of the evening to you," I said to Jo.

"Whatever," she answered.

"Look," I said, "if it's about kicking that kitten…"

"Huh?"

"Inside joke," I said. "Very inside. Forget I said anything."

I tugged twice on the rope.

"We've got ten seconds to clear," I told Jo. "The grappling hook is coming down."

We both stepped back a healthy distance. There was a slight thump as the rope hit the grass in front of us.

Jo stepped forward to reel in the rope and wind it up to place in her backpack.

As she completed that task, I stayed where I was. Much as Raven's attitude bothered me, I had to admit it was amazing to watch her climbing abilities.

She threaded her way back down the outer wall of the hospital, finding nooks and crevices in the bricks.

Halfway down, she froze. She gave a warning hiss.

That's when the flicker of a flashlight to my left caught my eye. With her bird's-eye view, she'd spotted it first.

The light moved and bobbed with the rhythm of a man at a walking pace. Security guard.

At this point, he didn't seem to be hurrying. The light flicked around as he checked doors and windows. But that lack of purpose would only last about thirty seconds. This guy wasn't a slacker—he was flashing the light up and down the walls. Chances were too good that he'd pin Raven with that light.

I was guessing Raven didn't want to move because she was afraid it would catch his eye.

"Jo," I said in a low voice. "Trouble."

She saw it immediately. "We need to distract him."

"We could make out," I said.

"What?"

"You know. Like in movies. We could start kissing and look all passionate, like we didn't notice the guard, and then be all embarrassed about being caught, and that would distract him from Raven above us. It's a price I'm willing to pay."

"Make out," she said. "Kiss."

"It's a sacrifice I'm prepared to make for the team," I said.

"I'd hate to make you pay a price that high," she said. "Let's try something else."

She stepped back, then started screaming, "Get away from me! I don't know you!"

"What?" I stepped forward and grabbed her arm.

She grabbed mine in return, twisted it and flipped me to the ground. The air rushed from my lungs. Standing over me, she yelled, "You're disgusting! Slimeball!"

Then she turned and ran, leaving me alone with the guard coming up fast on the sidewalk.

"Hey!" the guard shouted. "What's going on!"

"I dated a creep, that's what's wrong!" she shouted without slowing down. "He's back there by the bushes!"

The flashlight beam swung in my direction. But by then I was already running too. Opposite direction.

FOURTEEN

Seven o'clock on Saturday night, and I stepped into the ring for the fifth fight on the card. There was a good crowd in Billy's gym, and the air was heavy with sweat, fear, aggression and tension.

This was amateur night, and Billy was showcasing the best of his teenage fighters against a boxing club up from Seattle. We didn't have the home-crowd advantage. Seattle was close enough to Vancouver that a busload of fans had made the journey, and they were doing their best to out-cheer and out-jeer the friends and family of our hometown kids.

With the referee at the center, I touched gloves with my opponent, Alex Meunster. He was big and brawny. No surprise, his nickname was "The Monster." Although we were in the same weight category, much of my muscle was in my upper thighs. I could run forever. I told myself I would be faster and more intelligent than him, and in my mind I was Muhammad Ali facing George Foreman.

Meunster the Monster wore his hair long enough that it was bound in a ponytail. He had tattoos across his gleaming pectorals and massive biceps. Crude tattoos. Like he'd had them done in juvie. Not cool, expensive tattoos like the ones curling around my left shoulder.

His grin—blue because of his mouthguard—was more like the leer of someone with a big appetite about to dig into a buffet.

Billy had prepped me. This guy wanted to throw the glamorous knockout punch, and he was 20 and 0 with that strategy. And I had no intention of being his buffet.

The bell rang and he moved in. I didn't bounce on my feet, signaling what he expected, as I am sure he'd been prepped on my fighting style. He figured I'd be looking to counterpunch my way out, dodging his punches and looking for a big right-hander to take him out when he got tired.

Nope. Not this time. I'd already decided my strategy. We'd all been trained to throw the hard punches. Day after day at the heavy bag, that's what we did, until our upper arms ached as much as our knuckles throbbed. Instead, to confuse his defenses, my strategy was to use something he probably hadn't seen before. Light punches.

First, it would set me up for harder punches later. Second, light punches can be thrown from a wider range of positions and movements. Unlike a power punch, a light punch doesn't need you to be perfectly balanced or grounded. The lighter punches wouldn't hurt him, but he was going to be seeing lots of them—and feeling them—from a lot of different angles.

As he closed in, I leaned backward and jabbed, a movement that threw me farther backward and took power out of the punch. But it popped him on the cheekbone, and I saw his eyes flare open in surprise.

I knew it hadn't hurt him, but he'd reacted. I had surprised him. That was my goal. I was trying to make him fearful of getting hit, even though none of my hits would do any damage.

That was the pattern of the first round. I wasn't thinking punch. I was thinking touch and slap, like I was trying to knock a bug out of the air. With each exhalation, I extended a jab. Left, right. Falling backward to dodge a big swing or ducking beneath a haymaker, I made sure that I kept flicking my hands in his direction.

Because I wasn't throwing power into those punches, it took very little energy. I could do this for five rounds and be as fresh as when I started.

The bell ended the first round, and he was breathing hard as he went to his corner. I'd succeeded in puffing a point on his cheekbone, and he'd landed a heavy body blow to my right side that I knew would bruise later.

In the corner, Billy wiped my face with a wet towel and said only three words: "I like it."

I nodded.

When the bell rang for the second round, Meunster took three hard strides toward me. He was irritated. Perfect.

Time to see if I'd softened him up. I made a quick jerking movement with my right shoulder. Didn't throw a punch. Just that slight movement. It stopped him briefly.

That's when I knew I had him. He was reacting to anything I did, worried about my hands and where the next punch would come from. He believed I had punching power from anywhere, when the truth was anything I did from my off-balance positions would have been no worse than a friend poking him unexpectedly.

My intent for the next half of the round was to alternate between throwing those fast light punches and faking punches. And then, because I didn't want him to have a chance to talk things over with his coach after the second round, I was going to use the last half of this round for a complete strategy switch. I wanted to take advantage of his confused defenses and work on the five-punch combo that Ali had used to set up Foreman for the big punch.

It didn't happen that way.

"Get him, Jace!" came a distinctive voice from the crowd. My father. The world-famous neurosurgeon. Beloved by all except his wife and his own two sons.

Impossible that he knew I was here tonight. This was my secret alternative world.

I couldn't help but glance over. He was in the second row from the front.

Impossible.

And sitting right beside my father was Jo. Holding an iPhone sideways as she videoed the fight.

What was she doing with him?

And what kind of message was my father trying to send me by announcing his presence here? That he—

I never got a chance to finish the thought. Not until later in the evening, as I headed into the locker room to shower and change.

Because interrupting my thoughts was a nuclear bomb that exploded against the side of my head. I didn't even realize I was on the mat until that familiar whoosh of nitrate to the brain came with Billy popping open smelling salts below my nostrils and telling me I was an idiot.

Billy was correct. I was an idiot for letting anything distract me.

With the fight, Meunster the Monster had gained a 21 and 0 record, and all I'd gotten out of it was two loosened front teeth, a headache of biblical proportions and questions that wouldn't go away about my father and Jo.

There was one other thing I'd gained—a message in my jacket pocket: *You know the Denny's. Eleven PM. Be alone and waiting.*

FIFTEEN

Same Denny's as before. Same location where I'd once believed no one from the mansion world would ever see me.

But my faith had been shaken by seeing my own father in the stands during my fight. How had he discovered that I lived a separate life, where the world was gritty and real and people didn't solve their problems by hiring other people to take care of the dirty work?

And what had Jo been doing there with him?

Instead of salad and water, I ordered two hamburgers and two chocolate milk-shakes and left my full glass of water untouched on the table. There was no point in trying to keep my weight down for the next week or two. I could always work it off later.

When the hamburgers and shakes arrived, I was still alone, facing the door on the opposite side of the booth and still wondering who had left the note in my pocket. The person who'd burned my hands with curling irons? Or Raven and Jo? Or, as I still half suspected, were they one and the same?

I was just finishing my second chocolate shake when Raven and Jo pulled open the door and walked inside, scanning in both directions with their usual feral alertness.

They sat across from me in the booth.

Jo broke the silence. "Never thought you'd get up from the mat. That dude smoked you. In the video on my phone, I keep replaying that bomb that knocked you on your butt, and every time I hear the impact of his glove against your face, I smile all over again."

"How about we move past the social niceties?" I said. "Why were you there with my father?"

"Why have you lied to us?" Raven said. Her eyes were intense with anger. "That Mustang was a rental. You had me break into your own family's vacation house. You've been playing us from the beginning."

But I was just as angry. "You promised you'd both be out of my life after the hospital. I did my part to run and distract the security guard. You escaped. I didn't ask you back into my life. So why don't you both leave? Starting now."

Raven answered by pulling her phone out of her pocket. She entered her password to unlock it and slid it across to me. "Hit *Play*."

The video player was set up on the phone, so I did.

I saw a grainy image of me sliding through the window of Dr. Evans's office. I pushed the phone back at her.

"So," Raven said. "We talk. You listen. You follow commands. Or that's the video that reaches people who can hurt you."

I'd already been back in Dr. Evans's office. As Jace Wyatt, the smiling, nice son of the hospital's most beloved surgeon. I'd already taken the video-cam pens and downloaded all the video.

"May I?" I asked as I pulled the phone back to me.

I took her silence as a sign of consent. I pulled up the YouTube app and found a link to a video that I'd posted on my private channel. I tapped the link and waited for the video to upload.

I pushed the phone back to her. Jo leaned in and watched with Raven. Both were seeing some artful cut and splice. First came Raven's voice from the base of the hospital wall.

"Jo is here to stand guard, so that means you can climb and bring down the risk factor for me. If I go up alone, all you're risking is whether you can outrun a cop or security guard while I'm stuck on the wall. With you on the wall with me and we get caught, all we need to do is ditch the painting and pretend it was some kind of urban-climbing stunt dare."

Then came equally grainy video of Raven lifting the window to break into Dr. Evans's office, taken from the pen I'd left behind earlier that same day when I'd gone in to make sure the window was unlatched.

I had carefully edited myself out of the videos.

Both of them glared at me.

I smiled as I spoke. "I've got some software rigged so that if I don't put in a special password every twenty-four hours, this link goes public, and all the people who matter will get an email inviting them to the YouTube link."

Life, to me, was a combination of chess and boxing. You had to think everything through a couple of moves ahead and also be prepared to punch hard and often.

"You might think your video against mine makes for a stalemate," I said. "But that would be incorrect. Given the sordid past that each of you has tried so hard to avoid, the authorities would be a lot tougher on you than on me. And even if the authorities wanted to come down hard on me, I can access a lot better legal help than you can."

Each of them showed a face as rigid as those of some of the old women at my father's tennis club who'd had too many shots of Botox.

"So," I said, "tell me again the part where you talk and I listen and follow commands? That will give me a chance to tell you both to kiss my—"

"Raven and I followed him," Jo said. "Your father. We had your house staked out."

"One of your houses, silver-spoon boy," Raven said, her voice dripping with disgust. "Not so easy, deciding where you might be. The uptown luxury condo?

Perhaps the West Vancouver mansion. Or the vacation property a half hour down the road on the coast."

"Don't forget Paris and New York," I said. "And Hawaii. Then it's a private-helicopter ride to the private jet, and foot massages the entire flight. It would be far too stressful to land without relaxed feet."

Raven grabbed my full glass of water and threw it into my face.

It was satisfying to see how I had pushed her buttons.

"We through here?" I said as I began to stand, letting the water run down my face as if it didn't exist.

"Sure," Jo said. "As long as you don't want to know what we found out about your father. And a detective named Vince Crowther."

I sat.

As they say, that was *check* and *mate*. With me watching my king topple across the board.

SIXTEEN

When Jo smiled at my sudden lurch back into the booth, it didn't appear to be tainted by the vindictive triumph that I'd been happy to focus on them.

"We really do have information you want and need," Jo said. "If the two of you can behave in a civilized manner, maybe we can get all of this sorted out. And Raven and I need it sorted out, because we don't want any of the crap that lands on you to fall on us."

Jo turned to Raven. "We are both mad at his feeble attempts to play us, but I think the key thing to realize is that when he thought he had us because of his videos, all he did with that leverage was ask us to leave him alone. Nothing more. I think that means he passed the test. We can trust him."

"Look, he was a sneak, shooting that video."

"Hypocrisy," I said, "thy name is Raven."

Jo said to Raven, "He has a point. He did it to protect himself—we did the same for us, for the same reason. He's clumsy, but at least he thinks like us. Wouldn't you rather be working with someone who has the beginnings of street smarts?"

"I just don't like his attitude," Raven said.

"Yeah," Jo said. "He's a rich kid. Get over it. He's also a rich kid who doesn't whine when his hands hurt or when someone beats the crap out of him in a boxing match. He doesn't make excuses either."

"Actually," I said, "I had the guy where I wanted him until I looked over and saw you in the stands."

Jo said to Raven, "So he makes excuses. All of us do."

"He thinks he's pretty," Raven said. "I don't like that either."

"Um," I said, "I'm right here. I'm not deaf."

"Well," Jo said to Raven, "he is pretty in a brooding kind of way, so get over that too."

"Still here," I said. "Across the booth from both of you."

Raven said to Jo, "He's not that smart. And he's so not smart, he thinks I'm not smart. There were so many red flags when he faked like we were breaking into someone else's home."

"Blah, blah, blah," Jo said. "I've heard it a dozen times. He didn't do anything about the video camera. You saw him from the window, chatting with the private security. He left the rental-car papers in the glove box. What can you expect? He lives in a mansion, not a homeless shelter. Some things take time to learn."

Raven crossed her arms.

I crossed mine. I didn't feel dignified, however. My shirt was soaked.

"Raven," Jo said, "someday down the road, a guy like him could help us. And his brother can help. Right now he needs what we have. And I think he'll honor an agreement to help us later if we help him now. So reach across and shake his hand, and later I'll let you watch my video so you can enjoy the part of the fight where the dude smokes him and knocks him on his butt."

I made the first move and held out my hand.

Raven stared, blinked and then shook my hand. But didn't let go. She squeezed hard, probably guessing how much it would hurt my blisters, and said, "I'm not doing this for you. I'm doing it for Jo. You mess with us again and I'll sneak into your room at night and mess you up so bad you won't know if you're a boy or a girl."

"I think you're pretty too," I said.

For a split second, a smile struggled to break loose on her face, but she stomped it out in time with a glare.

"Why did you lie to me about the vacation place?" Raven said.

"Still don't know who put my hands on curling irons," I said. "You guys showed up at a time that was a little too convenient. I needed your help, but I didn't want to give you leverage knowing it was my house."

"It didn't work," Raven said. "It only made us dig deeper."

"I know that now," I said. "But I still don't know whether it was the two of you in the gym trying to crack me and see if I'd spill your names. Secrecy seems like the way you operate."

"It wasn't us," Jo said. "We only have one question for you. What made you want our help?"

"To learn about my father," I said.

"What I meant," Jo said, "was why now? You must have had questions about him for a while."

I thought about whether I should trust them. "An anonymous email directed me to look into my father's activities."

This was not the time and place to mention that Bentley and I had learned it came from our mother, and that we still didn't know why she'd sent it, or why she'd sent it anonymously.

"Why?"

"Don't know," I said. Which was disturbingly true. Why had our own mother done this? "Not yet. But when I learn what my father did, I'll probably be able to figure out who wanted him caught."

"Fair enough," Jo said.

"Tell me," I said, "why were you at the boxing match with my father?"

Raven said, "GPS devices on him and Bentley. Easy to plant on your father's car in the hospital parking lot, and easy to plant in your brother's backpack. We wanted to track their movements to find out exactly what you were up to."

"Your father," Jo said, "has had you followed by a private detective. Yesterday we followed him to the investigator's office, and then we followed the investigator following you."

"Vince Crowther."

"Yeah," Jo said. "Know him?"

"Hired him," I said. "Obviously, he decided he could make more money by letting my father know what I was trying to do."

I glared at Raven. "Before you call me an idiot, I didn't let him know I was Jace Wyatt. I made him think I was just a kid trying to make it as a boxer."

"Not guessing he'd look into your background anyway? Wouldn't take much to figure out who you are," said Raven.

"Looking back, I realize that," I said, knowing how weak it sounded.

"Lesson learned," Jo said. "Now you understand why Raven and I trust no one. That's why tonight we tracked your father to the fight. He didn't know who I was, so I sat beside him. In case he made a phone call that I could overhear. We were also worried he might try something again to hurt you."

"Again?" I said.

"What if he was the one who put the curling irons on you?"

Maybe, I thought. His showing up at the fight to let me know he knew about my secret life was obviously an unspoken threat.

"Flash back to me descending the hospital wall," Raven said. "We need to get to the point. I'm nervous here. Who knows how else Jace lets himself get tracked?"

Jo grinned at me. "Flash back to me introducing you to the ground, then sending the guard your way. Best distraction plan, huh? And isn't it the kind of stuff the best memories are made of?"

"Huh," I said.

"All along," Raven said, "it had been our plan to return later that night and break back into Evans's office. He's chief of staff. I wanted to learn what I could about your father. Try to find what you were looking for before you found it. Because if you were messing with us, that would be protection."

"Huh," I said.

"So with you scrambling to escape the security guard, all I did was climb back up into the office. You had those video-cam pens pointing at Evans's desk, so it didn't catch me on video. I dropped a cloth over the pens so movement wouldn't trigger the automatic cameras, and then I searched around. Ready for something ironic?"

"Why not?" I said. I didn't want her to know how intensely curious I was.

"In an age of technology, where the first thing we think of is hacking a computer," she said, "sometimes the safest place to store information is in a filing cabinet. On paper. Right, Jo?"

Jo reached behind her back and pulled out two folders that she'd kept hidden beneath her jacket.

"You owe us," Jo said. "Someday, we'll be back to collect. I trust you. So don't let me down."

Jo slid the folders across to me.

I left the folders unopened as they stood up from the booth. They left Denny's without a backward glance.

SEVENTEEN

I stood behind Dr. Evans's desk the next morning. His smug perspective on the world was obvious to me in the enlarged trophy photos scattered across the opposite wall. Every time he looked up, he would see himself in smiling poses with various celebrities or high-profile politicians, including the prime minister of Canada.

I'd never liked this man, and over the years I'd had plenty of occasions to hone my dislike. He and his wife were constant visitors to our vacation home on the coast-line. He dressed out of a fashion magazine and had a habit of snorting laughter at his own jokes and constantly smoothing his thinning hair over his scalp whenever he was nervous.

"Private YouTube channel," he said, watching the computer screen as he waited for the URL to load. I'd just explained what we would be viewing. "Interesting."

That was another habit that irritated me. He always said *interesting* when he didn't understand something.

Well, he'd understand soon enough. I'd uploaded some great video.

"Hey," he said as the clip started to play. "That's my office and…"

He was picking his nose. This had taken place later in the morning, after he'd hidden the Picasso. Just in case the footage of him with a stolen Picasso wasn't enough leverage to get what I wanted, I knew he'd be mortified if I threatened to release a clip of him digging in his left nostril.

"Yup," I said. "It gets better. Or worse, depending on your viewpoint."

With four video-cam ballpoints in the penholder, I'd gotten a lot of great footage of Dr. Evans. I stood behind him as we both reviewed the edited montage. First he picked up the painting and examined it from all angles. Then he moved to a filing cabinet and hid it inside a drawer. Later, he slipped it into a briefcase. Then, in the last bit of footage, he was seen leaving his office with the briefcase.

The video ended.

I moved out from behind his desk, pulled up a chair and sat across from him.

"I assume you're behind this illegal video of a private office," Dr. Evans said. "My advice is to delete the video immediately before I call in the authorities."

"My advice is to help me with what I need. Otherwise that video is going to be a great embarrassment for you."

"I was rubbing my nose," he said. He ran his fingers through his hair and smoothed it over his scalp. "From a different angle, that would be obvious."

"That would be the least of your worries. The Picasso you took from the office is real."

"Of course it is," he said. "I had it authenticated and valued."

"You know where it's from?" I said.

"Your vacation house. Where it hung on the east wall of the dining room."

This was troubling me. That he didn't seem troubled.

"Exactly," I said. "How many times during dinner parties did you make it clear to everyone that you lusted over that painting and would do anything to own it?"

"Every time I was there," Dr. Evans said.

"So there are plenty of witnesses to agree to that if it comes before a judge."

"I suppose," he said.

It bothered me that he wasn't running his hands over his head.

"So," I said. "When it's discovered that you have the real one and that the

123

Picasso hanging in our dining room is a forgery..."

It was a forgery painted by Jo and planted by Raven. But that truth would never make it into a courtroom.

"Hmm," he said. "I suppose that would make it awkward for your father."

"Excuse me?" I said.

"What game are you trying to play here?" he asked. "Tell me, and maybe I can help."

I fought the urge to run my fingers through my own hair. This wasn't going the way I'd expected. Bentley and I had known it was a medium-long shot in the first place, but now it looked like all chances of leverage were disappearing.

"It's simple," I said. "There's a forgery in our vacation house. You're on video in obvious possession of the original. And furthermore, I've been recording our entire conversation with this pen..."

I pulled out the miniature cam, which had been peeking over the edge of my shirt pocket. There were three in his penholder too, just in case.

"And the video from this pen," I continued, "will clearly show you admitting that you took the painting and had it authenticated and valued. I'd say if I brought this new video and the YouTube video to the authorities, it would be obvious that you stole the Picasso you've always wanted and replaced it with a forgery. Life as you know it would be over. Bye-bye nice office and nice home."

It was a bluff. I had no intention of seeing anyone charged with a crime that didn't happen. Although, if Dr. Evans had any degree of honesty, he wouldn't have taken and hidden the Picasso that had been waiting for him on his desk.

"Interesting," he said. Hands still calm on his lap. "And why are you making this threat?"

"I want information from you," I said. "About my father."

"So you're blackmailing me."

"Trading," I said. I thought about it. "Nope. Might as well call it what it is. I'm blackmailing you for help."

"What kind of information about your father?"

I had the information in one of the folders that Raven had taken from Dr. Evans's office.

"About two weeks after my brother was born," I said, "my father faced a private disciplinary hearing at the hospital. The records show it was for harassing a nurse, and that there was a settlement. I doubt that's what happened. I think Croft money was used to protect him. I want to know what really happened."

"I don't think you do," Dr. Evans said. "Really. You should just drop this."

"I want answers," I said. "Or the videos go to the hospital board."

He sighed. "The irony here is so delicious."

I squinted in puzzlement.

He answered my unspoken question.

"There's a reason I always said I wanted that painting," Dr. Evans said. "It's because of what I know about your father. I said it as often as possible, in front of as many people as possible, because it was a constant reminder to him that I owned him."

"You owned him?" I'm sure I looked as puzzled as I felt. Dr. Evans was definitely in the power position here.

Dr. Evans gave me a tight grin. "It's called blackmail. When the painting showed up on my desk, I thought he'd left it behind for me to finally get me off his back."

Now I felt my jaw unhinge.

Dr. Evans snorted. "So here's the truth. The best thing you could do is leave that fake in place and never let anyone know about the switch. Because the only person it's really going to hurt is your father."

What Dr. Evans didn't know was that was the most valuable thing I could have heard. I dreamed of hurting my father.

"So," I said, "if you now have the painting you always wanted, why not tell me the truth about the disciplinary hearing?"

EIGHTEEN

Schmedley—the detective Bentley and I had hired whose real name was Vince Crowther—had a decent office high up in an office building that gave a good view of downtown Vancouver. By decent, I didn't mean expensive carpet and oil paintings and a gleaming walnut desk, but rather clean and organized, with classy print reproductions of famous artists.

He was expecting me at 10:00 AM, and that's when I opened the door to the office.

I held a throwaway cell phone in my right hand, all set up with a month-to-month cell and data plan purchased from Walmart. I truly did mean to throw it away as soon as this meeting was finished.

"Good to see you," Schmedley said. He didn't even bother to get up. He remained in his chair in front of his computer and swiveled to face me. Sloppy.

He probably meant what he said, that it was good to see me.

That's because I'd promised to bring him a certified check for payment for his services. I held it in my left hand and walked forward and set it on his desk.

"Thanks," he said. But not until he'd looked it over thoroughly to make sure it was full payment.

"In the legal world," I said as I backed away a few steps, "proof is whatever will hold up in court. Isn't that what you told me when I hired you?"

"Exactly."

"So if someone threatened you, and you had it on video, that would be proof."

"Yup," he said. He was a private investigator.

"And that would make it probable," I continued, "that you record all conversations in this office with a hidden video camera?"

He was a detective; he would have all the latest in electronic surveillance equipment.

"Thinking of threatening me?" he said, smirking.

His non-answer was as good as an answer. Bentley's prediction had been correct. It would have been stupid to march in and make threats that could get me in trouble later. Which meant, of course, that Bentley and I had needed to come up with a way to hurt Schmedley without any chance of repercussions for us.

I glanced at my throwaway phone. I had an email in the out-box, and I hit *Send*.

"So if a person had been tortured by having curling irons taped to his hands," I said, "he'd have a tough time getting justice without proof of who had done it to him."

I was watching Schmedley's face carefully. I was glad when he gave me a smile. To me, that said far more than all the evidence Bentley had found by hacking the guy's computer. The trouble with the evidence on Schmedley's computer was that it wouldn't hold up in court, because it had been illegally obtained.

"Very tough time," Schmedley answered.

His computer dinged. Incoming email. From me.

Bentley and I had been undecided. Would he glance at the screen, or would he be polite and ignore it? I'd guessed he wouldn't be polite. Not to a kid like me.

He glanced at the screen to check his message. The subject heading was all in caps: *PROOF OF CURLING IRON TORTURE*.

We'd been prepared in case he didn't look. I'd have told him I'd just sent him an email and asked him to look at it. That would sound innocent on whatever recording equipment he had in the office.

The important thing was the satisfaction of him knowing that Bentley and I were paying him back.

He looked at the screen and looked at me.

I shrugged. That would look innocent on a video recording of this conversation.

He would have been inhuman not to be curious enough to open the email.

As the attachments downloaded and began to open on Schmedley's monitor, I hit *Send* on a text in my phone that had been waiting to go to Bentley. The text had one word: *ENJOY*.

Bentley had a monitor at his end to mirror what was on Schmedley's monitor. Getting into Schmedley's hard drive a day earlier had been a breeze for Bentley. He'd set up an email account that was almost identical to Winchester's. Since Schmedley had already been in email contact with Winchester, he wouldn't get suspicious receiving an email supposedly from Winchester. Nor would Schmedley have any reason to distrust the attachment.

The email had this for a subject heading: *To Confirm. This is Jace.*

The attachment had looked like a photo of me but had also been an executable file that slid into Schmedley's computer system. Malware. From there, Bentley had taken full control of Schmedley's hard drive. That's where we'd found plenty of proof that it had been Schmedley who'd put the curling irons on me.

Right now on Schmedley's monitor, the first photo in the PowerPoint slide show I had just emailed him popped into view. I'd been in a hurry, so there were no fancy transitions between photos, and the photos weren't perfect, but I was confident the slide show would make my point.

The first photo in the slide show was a piece of paper hanging from a fishing line, against the background of the cubicle door in the toilet in the gym where Schmedley had duct-taped me in place. All the rest would look the same, but with a different message.

THERE IS NO ONE AROUND TO HEAR YOU SCREAM

Schmedley glanced over his shoulder at me.

"Looks familiar," I said. "How about to you?"

I was being careful not to say anything that could incriminate me if it was played to a jury in a courtroom.

"I don't know what you are talking about," Schmedley said. He must have been just as aware of the danger of having this conversation recorded.

"Keep reading," I said.

BECAUSE THE PAIN WILL BE FAR WORSE THAN CURLING IRONS

"Looks like an amateur attempt," Schmedley said. "Are you wearing a recording device?"

I smiled for the benefit of whatever camera was here.

"All I wanted to do," I said, "was drop off the payment, like I promised. I hope you discover that I've paid you back in full."

His eyes returned to the screen. And to the PowerPoint file, where he could see the next photo of a note hanging from a fishing line.

WE KNOW YOU WENT TO MY FATHER AND LET HIM HIRE YOU TO FIND OUT WHY I'D HIRED YOU TO LOOK INTO THE DISCIPLINARY HEARING

"Speaking of needing proof in court," Schmedley said, "incriminating emails can be traced."

"Yes," I said. "They can."

Hence the throwaway.

DID YOU DO THAT BECAUSE YOU THOUGHT YOU COULD MAKE A LOT MORE MONEY OFF HIM THAN OFF ME?

"Libel is also a criminal act," Schmedley said. "Libel consists of an accusation that hurts someone's reputation and that can be proven in a court of law."

"Absolutely," I said. "And what accusation would that be? We are just having a conversation here, and I can't quite follow it. So please—explain. What accusation have I made against you?"

"Nice try," he said.

"Something happening on your monitor?" I asked.

AFTER ALL, UNTIL YOU LEARNED I WAS HIS SON, YOU THOUGHT I WAS JUST SOME INNER-CITY KID TRYING TO SCORE WITH SOME KIND OF BLACKMAIL

He flipped me the bird.

"I notice that you are distracted by incoming emails," I said. "I can leave if you want. Or we can continue to discuss all of your services. And I mean all of them."

I pointed at his monitor, where I knew the next photo on the cubicle door would appear as part of the PowerPoint file he had opened. A photo of a note he knew I had written for him to read.

HOW DO I KNOW IT WAS YOU? REMEMBER THE NOTES YOU SHOWED ME WHILE I WAS DUCT-TAPED TO A TOILET? NOTES PRINTED FROM A COMPUTER INSTEAD OF HANDWRITTEN? YOU WROTE THE SEQUENCE OF NOTES ON YOUR COMPUTER. TRASHING FILES DOESN'T DELETE FILES. YOU HAVE TO OVERWRITE THE LOCATION ON THE HARD DRIVE WITH ANOTHER FILE.

"I'm wondering," I said. "Have you ever stored inappropriate photos of yourself on your hard drive? Because that would be embarrassing if people saw you in a different light, wouldn't it? If they saw you doing very private things that aren't socially appropriate."

AS YOU ARE READING THIS, YOUR EMAIL PROGRAM HAS SENT OUT A PHOTO OF YOU TO EVERY CONTACT IN YOUR ADDRESS BOOK. YOU'LL HAVE TO GUESS WHICH PHOTO. BUT THERE WERE A LOT TO CHOOSE FROM THAT MAKE YOU LOOK BAD. REALLY BAD.

I could see by Schmedley's face that Bentley and I had scored a direct hit. His sloppy pale face turned even paler.

"Enjoying the conversation?" I said. "You don't want to miss any of it."

WE HAD FULL ACCESS TO YOUR COMPUTER. AND THE BACKUP DRIVE ATTACHED TO IT. AND FULL ACCESS TO THE CLOUD WHERE YOU HAD BACKED IT UP IN CASE YOUR HARD DRIVE FAILED. WHEN YOU SEE THE CLOWN FACE ON YOUR SCREEN, THE SOFTWARE PROGRAM TO DESTROY ALL YOUR DATA HAS JUST COMPLETED ITS

TASK, INCLUDING THE DELETION OF ALL YOUR EMAILS ON YOUR SERVER.

It took him a while to absorb that message. I was okay waiting. Putting it on the computer monitor meant that this conversation couldn't be recorded. And that Bentley and I had the satisfaction of letting him know we knew what he'd done.

His expression was a combination of anger and horror when he turned back to me.

"It's a dangerous world," I said. "I sure appreciate your help in learning how dangerous it can be. Think others might hire you in the future?"

Again I pointed at the screen. "You seem distracted by emails. Don't worry about me. Go ahead and read whatever has been sent to you."

I felt savage satisfaction. He had no doubt whatsoever that the silent, onscreen conversation was everything I wanted to say to him out loud in his office.

WE HAVE YOUR DATA. IT WOULD BE BEST IF YOU DIDN'T LOOK FOR WORK AGAIN. FUTURE CLIENTS WILL GET EMAILS LETTING THEM KNOW WHAT YOU DID TO FORMER CLIENTS.

"Only one thing remains," I said.

I waited for the clown face on his monitor. The clown face telling him that he'd just lost his professional life's worth of information and that Bentley and I owned it, along with those incriminating photos of himself.

THERE WILL BE NO ONE AROUND TO HEAR YOU SCREAM. BECAUSE I AM GOING NOW.

The monitor went totally black except for a closeup of a grinning clown. Revenge. But revenge that left no proof it was me or Bentley.

I waved my fingers at Schmedley. And left him alone so that no one could hear him scream.

NINETEEN

All was in place for a cheerful family gathering in the living room, beneath oil paintings of the generations of Croft men whose predatory assaults on the natural resources of British Columbia over the past 150 years had yielded the family wealth. One of the portraits was so large it had a set of drapes that could protect it from sunlight so that the oils wouldn't sustain cumulative damage. On this morning, the drapes were bunched open, revealing the original Albert Croft.

"Shall I ring for more tea?" my mother asked, sitting neatly on the couch with her knees pressed together and slightly sideways. Behind her, from the massive portrait, Albert looked sternly down, as if assessing whether her social niceties would reach his standards. "Winchester?"

I held back a sigh. My life—from the oil portraits to the little silver bell she held ready to summon a maid—was a cliché. Hypocrite that I was, I sipped at a glass of freshly squeezed orange juice from the breakfast tray that had just been delivered.

My father shook his head and refused to sit. He paced behind her couch. "I'm not interested in wasting much time this morning. Whatever Jace has called us to discuss needs to be finished by…"

He made a show of extending his left arm from his perfectly tailored suit so that he could look at his Daniel Roth Ellipsocurvex Tourbillon watch. All $150,000 worth of it. The semioval case was distinctive enough that anyone familiar with the world's most expensive watches would understand immediately what he was wearing. That excluded more than 99 percent of the population, which was one of the reasons to wear that kind of watch. Insiders liked having ways to signal status to other insiders, because that was the ultimate type of status: walking around with something so exclusive that the peasants couldn't understand how exclusive.

"This won't take long," I said. "It starts with asking why Mother would send me an anonymous email directing me to ask questions about what happened at the hospital when Bentley was born."

"What?" Mother said. Her voice held alarm.

"What?" Winchester said. His voice held anger.

I was sitting in a leather chair off to the side. I didn't want to be opposite Mother on the couch and my father pacing behind her. That would put me in direct line with my imperious ancestors and their misguided attempts at immortality via the oil paintings, and I was tired of seeing those ancestors and their smugness.

"Mother," I said. "It wasn't difficult to track down the source of the email. Heard of something called an IP address?"

"No," she said.

"Exactly," I said. "There's no doubt it came from your computer, but what I can't figure out is why you wanted me—or anyone—to dig up what happened at the hospital."

"Perhaps we do need tea," she said.

"My question is not going to go away," I said.

Winchester had stopped pacing and was staring at her with a peculiar intensity. It was obvious that he too wanted the answer.

She spoke in a brittle voice. "I've hated your father for a long time. That's no secret in this household. But divorce was not an option. There's a binding prenuptial in place, and without sufficient cause for divorce, it would have cost far more than I wanted the Croft fortune to lose."

She made sure to focus on me as she spoke, as if pretending Winchester wasn't in the room was a way to pretend he didn't even exist. "Your father is a clever, clever man. He's always had his eye on the bigger prize—the Croft fortune and all that it gives him. I'm sure he's been tempted many times to have an affair, but he knows that would trigger one of the clauses in the prenuptial agreement, and I'd be able to divorce him without a huge settlement."

Her smile became as brittle as her voice. "Ever since I was little, I was taught that the most important thing in my life was the Croft fortune. That nothing I did should ever threaten that legacy."

This was no surprise to me. I'd been taught the same thing.

"Another reason for a low-settlement divorce was if he committed a criminal act," she said. "Which he did at the hospital when Bentley was born. At the time, I didn't hate your father the way I do now. So I went along with it and was bound by a confidentiality agreement."

Understanding washed over me. "But if someone else revealed the criminal act, and it couldn't be proved you had led that someone else to knowledge about the crime, then you wouldn't be in legal trouble for breaking the agreement, and your divorce wouldn't drain anything from the Croft fortune."

"I don't deserve that scorn in your voice," she said. "Your life and Bentley's life would be much better without him in our lives. I have been a much better mother to you than Winchester has been a father. I refuse to ask forgiveness for sending that email and trying to expose him without it looking like I was behind it."

Just as I would refuse to ask her to apologize. We weren't that type of family.

"Then your tactic worked," I said. "Yes, I know what happened at the hospital.

But did you know that Dr. Evans has been blackmailing Father all these years because of it?"

Mother waved it away. "I suspected, but all I cared about was that the amount never increased. Evans didn't get greedy, and I was fine leaving that can of worms unopened. Instead, I'd rather hear from you what you discovered."

"Of course you would," I said. "It's going to save you about half a billion dollars."

"Think of it instead as taking that half billion away from your father," she said, as if he wasn't in the room. "Doesn't that make you feel better? So go ahead. Tell both of us what you know."

"How about we spare ourselves the dramatics," my father said as he reached into his suit jacket. He'd stopped pacing behind Mother. "Yes, after he was born I tried switching Bentley for another baby. It was obvious that he wasn't perfect. As I said then, I was just doing it to spare both of us. If I hadn't been caught, you would have never known. Just like the first time. Instead, we were saddled with Bentley for the rest of our lives."

Even after learning the truth from Dr. Evans, I still hadn't gotten over the emotional shock waves. To make sure the world believed his life was perfect, Winchester was willing to discard his own son and switch a baby at birth.

I was struggling to find a way to express my rage at this when, in one swift move, Winchester pulled out a hypodermic needle and jammed it into the meat of my mother's shoulder. With the sureness of the physician he was, he thumbed the plunger and injected her.

"Winchester," she said, slapping at her shoulder, "whatever are you expecting to accomplish with…"

Mother didn't get farther than that. She slumped to her side.

"I knew you'd found out," my father said to me.

"Yes," I said. "The detective. I have one question for you. Whose idea was it to put curling irons in my hands?"

"Curling irons?" He was obviously puzzled.

I detested myself for my relief. It told me that I still badly wanted a father to love, and that at least the man in front of me had not been willing to torture me.

"He tried to torture me to find out what you wanted to know," I said. "You should be more careful about the people you hire."

"As should you," he answered.

Touché.

I nodded. Or tried to nod.

He smiled at my slowing reactions. "Evans is a petty man. He took great satisfaction in calling me to tell me about your discussion with him. Instead, it served as a warning. I've been prepared for a meeting like this. Needle for your mother. Drugs in the orange juice for you."

I was fading fast.

"Night-night," my father said to me. "With both of you out, I'm sure I can rig some kind of accident that will take away all suspicion about your deaths."

I fought hard to remain conscious. I succeeded just long enough to see Bentley slip out from behind the drapes, holding a baseball bat.

That was ironic. If Bentley were any bigger, he wouldn't have been able to hide there.

With a mighty swing, he took out the side of my father's knee. Father screamed and fell sideways, clutching the shattered bone. No way would he walk without major surgery.

"Wow," Bentley said. "That felt good."

Then I was gone.

TWENTY

Two weeks later, on a sunny Saturday morning, I sat outside the old courthouse on Hornby Street that had been turned into the Vancouver Art Gallery. I wasn't interested in the gallery and its epic collection of Emily Carr paintings. I'd grown up with a scattering of her work in various homes. Nor was I interested in watching the jugglers or buskers nearby, or listening to a guy yell about why we needed to donate to an investigation of algae growth on whales in the wild.

I was focusing instead on the chessboard in front of me and the position of the pieces, highly aware of the chess clock beside the board. It has two timers, which only run one at a time. The way it works is simple. Make your move, then hit the button over your timer. This starts your opponent's timer. And vice versa. Run out of time, you lose.

My opponent and I had agreed on three minutes for the blitz chess match. Two twenty-dollar bills were under the board. We'd each contributed one bill, and the winner would take both.

I was hungry and needed the money more than the sunburned tourist in front of me. But he'd been better than I'd expected, and I was down to my final thirty seconds.

My queen was exposed, but protecting it would draw a knight.

My hope was that he wouldn't realize it quickly enough. I was down to twenty-five seconds.

As I made the move to protect my queen and slammed the timer button to start his count, I became vaguely aware of someone behind me. That was usual. Lots of people stopped to watch blitz chess. We were as much entertainment as the jugglers were. This was why I was here, hoping to fleece as many passersby as possible.

Sunburn hesitated, then made a bad move and hit the timer. I pounced, moving my queen. I was two moves from checkmate and victory.

Again he hesitated and made another bad move. I slid my queen to the right. He grimaced and toppled his king in surrender.

Then he gave me a sour look. "Always need help to win?"

"Huh?" I said.

"Nice try. Like you don't know those girls?"

I turned my head and saw Jo and Raven. No wonder the guy had been distracted. I had to admit, they looked good.

"I don't need them," I said, knowing they'd hear it too. I slid back his twenty. "Let's call it a draw."

I ignored Jo and Raven and gathered my pieces, folded my board and walked away with the board and the clock. I knew they'd follow, but this gave me the illusion of control.

"We'll find you again," Raven said from behind me. "Might as well hear us out. Remember, you owe us. And remember, we helped you because of how often you told us we owed you."

I moved to a bench. One sat on either side of me.

Jo said, "Want to tell us about your father?"

"You probably saw the headlines," I said. "He's been arrested. What more do you need?"

"You're right," she said. "It's your business. Not ours."

My business.

I'd learned that Dr. Winchester Wyatt had taken advantage of his position at the hospital and bribed the attending nurse and doctor at Bentley's C-section birth to switch Bentley with the baby of another woman who had delivered by C-section. That's what made it possible—the C-sections. Because the mothers didn't see and hold their babies until after the operation was complete.

What had exposed it almost immediately was a routine blood test that showed Bentley's blood type was wrong for the mother who thought he was her child. And when the questions began, the doctor and the nurse crumbled under pressure and confessed. It had taken a large amount of money to settle all of it—at least, an amount large for anyone but a Croft.

"I'm not here for gossip anyway," Jo said. "Straight up? We're here because Internet rumors have started about a team that is *living in the shadows, dispensing their own kind of justice.*"

Raven said, "That would be us. Someone sent out a message on a forum. A kid who needs help against authorities when other authorities won't help."

I said, "I think both of you need to look up the definition of *team*. Unless you mean just the two of you. If so, good luck and goodbye."

"For this kid to have any chance of retribution," Jo said, "we need you and your brother."

"We have our own troubles," I said.

"One computer hack from him, one social-situation scam from you. That's all we're asking. Then we'll leave you alone."

"What's in it for you two?" I asked. "Why take chances for someone else? Thought you liked being invisible."

Raven was serious and quiet as she spoke. "Hey, we all like to pretend we're cynical. But Jo and I realized that if you can make something better, you need to try. Injustice sucks."

"Feels good to fight it," Jo added. "I mean, some people recycle cans and bottles to feel good about themselves. What we're doing is just on a bigger scale.

As long as we stay invisible, we can take down people like your father." She pulled out her cell and showed me a text. "Bentley's in. Are you?"

Of course Bentley was in. He actually liked them.

What Jo didn't know was that Winchester Wyatt wasn't my father.

I hadn't been able to shake what Winchester had said when he thought he could get away with killing my mother and me, when he didn't know I had asked Bentley to hide in the drapes as backup.

After that, each night when I closed my eyes I heard Winchester's words again. *If I hadn't been caught, you would have never known. Just like the first time.*

The thing is, there was a 25 percent chance that the first baby born to Margaret Croft and Winchester Wyatt had also been born with the obvious features of a Laron-syndrome baby.

For years, I'd thought Winchester had not discovered that he and Margaret both carried the gene until Bentley was born. I was wrong.

I'd done my own blood test two days ago. Winchester wasn't my father. Margaret wasn't my mother.

You would have never known. Just like the first time.

Dr. Evans hadn't been blackmailing Winchester Wyatt for the failed switch of Bentley at birth. No. Dr. Evans had blackmailed Winchester about the *first* switch. Of me and the baby actually born into the Croft fortune, on the same day in the same hospital. I'd been born to a different mother.

Yes. The awful truth was that the first time, Winchester had succeeded in switching babies.

Someone out there was raising Bentley's real brother while I'd been given a silver spoon that I hated. Somewhere out there were my real father and mother.

I was messed up, knowing this. Maybe it wouldn't be a bad idea to stop feeling sorry for myself and help another kid get out of a situation that looked hopeless.

"I'm in," I told Raven and Jo. It flashed through my mind, the image of Bentley's tattoo on his right wrist and of mine on my right shoulder blade. Of us finding a way to give infinite possibilities to those who needed it most, and taking satisfaction from delivering knockout blows against corrupt authorities who were trying to take those possibilities away from them. "What do we do next?"

Yeah, I thought. I'm in. I stopped thinking about my sorrows and focused on something else. Infinite possibilities.

ACKNOWLEDGMENTS

Thanks to Andrew and everyone at Orca for their faith in this project.

With close to three million books in print,
SIGMUND BROUWER writes for both
children and adults but is happiest when
he is bucking authority. In the last ten
years, he has given writing workshops to
students in schools from the Arctic Circle
to inner-city Los Angeles. One of his latest
novels, *The Last Disciple*, earned Sigmund
an appearance on ABC Television's *Good
Morning America*. Sigmund and his
family live half of the year in Nashville,
Tennessee, and the other half in Red Deer,
Alberta. For more information, visit
www.sigmundbrouwer.com.